ROBERT MUCHAMORE'S
ROBIN HOOD

HACKING, HEISTS & FLAMING ARROWS

HOT
KEY
BOOKS

First published in Great Britain in 2020 by
HOT KEY BOOKS
80–81 Wimpole St, London W1G 9RE
www.hotkeybooks.com

A CIP catalogue record for this book is available from the British Library.

ISBN: 978-1-4714-0861-8
Also available as an ebook and in audio

1

Printed and bound in Great Britain by Clays Ltd, Elcograf S.p.A.

Hot Key Books is an imprint of Bonnier Books UK
www.bonnierbooks.co.uk

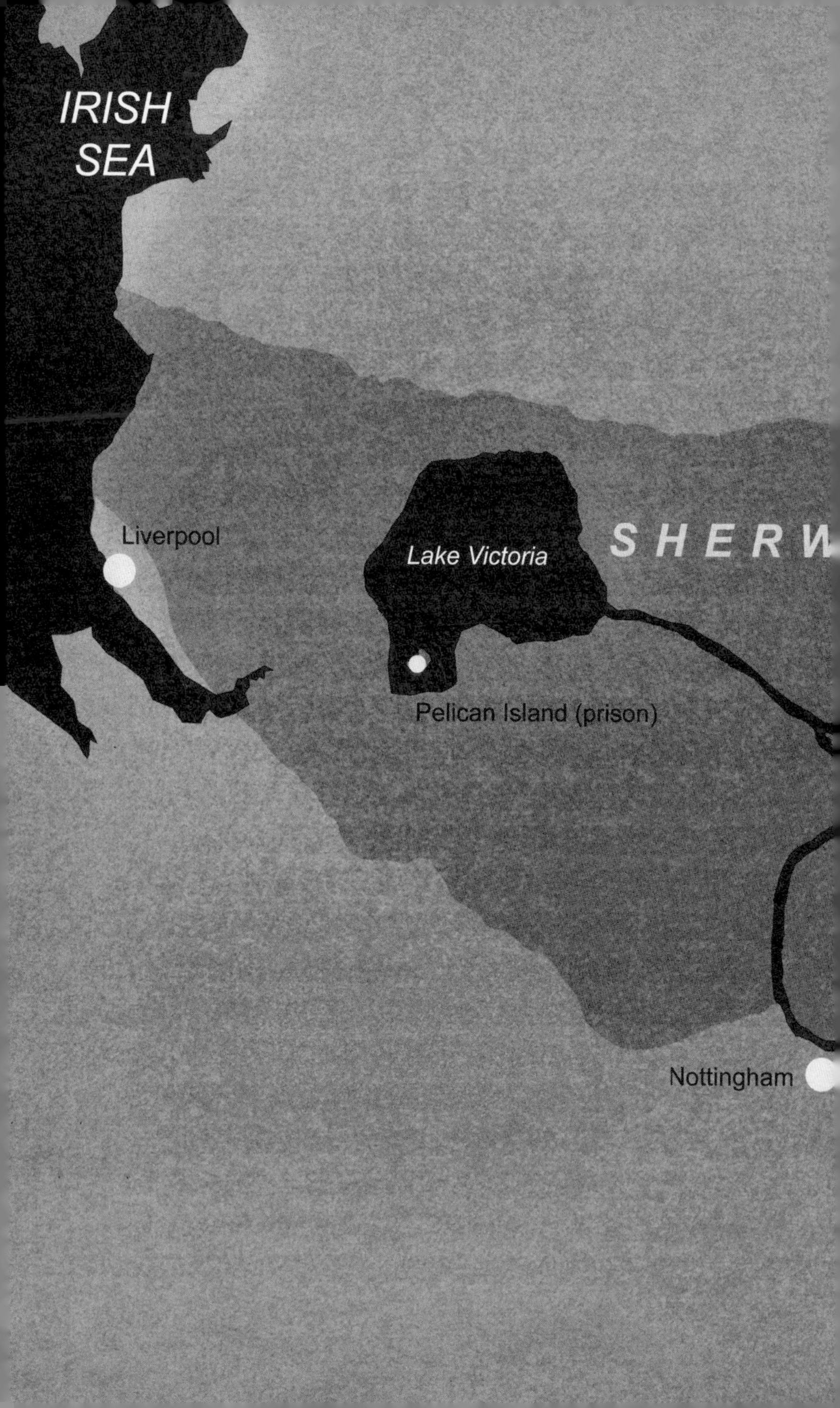
IRISH
SEA
Liverpool
Lake Victoria
S H E R W
Pelican Island (prison)
Nottingham

NORTH SEA

R24

Barnsdale

OD FOREST

Great Eastern Lakes

R24

Sherwood Castle

Sherwood Designer Outlets
(closed down)

Locksley

*Eastern
Delta*

R24

Capital City
(225 km)

AUTHOR'S NOTE

The characters in this book are fictional and a lot more bouncy than real people.

Please don't try to copy any of Robin's stunts.

Please don't shoot arrows at people or animals.

If you do try something stupid and wind up breaking your legs, don't come running to me.

ROBERT MUCHAMORE, 31ST APRIL 2020

1. MR BARCLAY IS A NUTTER

The legend of Robin Hood begins in Locksley High School, on a Wednesday afternoon. It was the middle of lunch break, and pepperoni pizza and buttered corn sat heavy in twelve-year-old Robin's nervous stomach.

'If we get caught, we're dead,' Robin's pal Alan Adale noted, as he shoulder-barged double doors.

The school was a dump and the boys set off down a corridor lined with vandalised lockers. Mildew on the windows gave the light a greenish tinge and a stink wafted from drains in the girls' bathroom at the far end.

The two lads were a contrast. Robin was small but muscly, with scruffy hair and ketchup down his purple school polo shirt. Alan was a neat freak. His gangly frame started with madly expensive basketball boots whiter than anything in a toothpaste ad and topped out with an extravagant afro that forced him to duck under doors.

'Mr Barclay is a nutter,' Alan continued. 'Craig got two weeks of detention for that burp in assembly.'

Robin smirked at the memory: Craig's vast rolling belch silencing a guest lecturing on water safety, and leaving half the school in hysterical laughter as Mr Barclay gripped Craig by his collar and dragged him out of the gym.

'Barclay's on lunch duty on the other side of the school,' Robin soothed. 'And you're just my lookout. All the benefit, none of the risk . . .'

Robin was trying to sound calm but shuddered when he stopped at a door. It had muddy kick-marks and peeling brown paint. The sign read *Mr Barclay – Head of Year Seven*, under which someone had graffitied: *Abandon hope ye who enter here.*

'Can you get me an A?' Alan begged, as Robin pulled a neon-yellow plastic key out of his pocket.

'Mate, you can barely add two numbers together.'

'Are you saying I'm thick?' Alan accused.

'Maths sure isn't one of your strengths,' Robin said diplomatically. 'Nobody's gonna believe you got an A.'

'How'd you get Barclay's key anyway?'

'He leaves his keys on the desk in his classroom,' Robin explained. 'I took a close-up photo, then made copies using the 3D printer at my dad's work.'

'My dad's got a 3D printer. He only used it once. So basically, he spent five hundred pounds to make a small plastic hedgehog.'

'Your family has *way* too much money,' Robin said irritably. 'Can we *please* concentrate . . .'

Keys are normally metal, so Robin worried as he slotted the yellow plastic inside the lock. Some girls ran out of the bathroom. There was a big shriek and one shouted, *Gimme my hat, moose brain!* But they paid the boys no attention.

Once they were out of sight, Robin twisted the key in the lock and felt it flex.

'I'm bigger, shall I try?' Alan asked.

'I don't want it to snap,' Robin explained. 'I'm being gentle . . .'

There was an alarming scraping sound, but just as Robin thought his efforts were doomed, the bolt made a satisfying *thunk*.

'Am I a genius, or what?' Robin said brightly. 'We're in!'

2. GOTTA KILL 'EM ALL

'You keep watch,' Robin told Alan, as he stepped into Mr Barclay's office. 'If anyone comes, bang on the door.'

'There's only one exit,' Alan said warily. 'The doors we came through.'

'It's only the second floor,' Robin explained. 'I can go out of the window.'

'What's my excuse for hanging out here, if someone asks?'

Robin sighed. 'Standing in a corridor isn't a crime. We talked this thorough already. Stop being a panic pants and let me work . . .'

Robin shook his head as he closed the office door. Recruiting Alan to be his lookout probably wasn't worth the earache, because if this went like the test run Robin did at home the night before, he'd get the job done in under eight minutes.

First Robin secured his emergency escape route, by grabbing two finger hooks and opening the rotting sash window. This let in fresh air, along with noise from older kids playing soccer in the courtyard below.

Barclay's office was a landfill site. Stacks of fat folders, dust-caked family photos, a musical *No. 1 Uncle* cookie jar with a smashed lid, and a wall clock that told the wrong time. The smell was a mix of Gazelle for Men body spray, a dandruff-speckled tracksuit top and the brie-and-tomato baguette mouldering in the bin.

After jiggling the mouse to make sure the desktop computer wasn't already switched on, Robin reached underneath the table and pushed the main power switch. He twisted back and forth in the office chair as the ancient Dell booted up.

'How much longer?' Alan asked, leaning in anxiously.

'I just got here,' Robin growled. 'Buzz off.'

The screen asked Robin for a staff ID and password.

Staff IDs were super-easy to find: they were written on the message boxes outside the staffroom, where kids could drop stuff like late homework or permission slips.

Barclay's password had made a meatier challenge, but Robin had captured it by installing a keylogger program on a laptop in his classroom. This small piece of software ran in secret, recording every keystroke made on the computer and sending a text file to Robin in a daily email.

After typing **4071** and **K1LLa11Year7s**, Robin waited for the Windows desktop to appear, then opened Locksley High's pupil database.

Robin had Mr Barclay's system password, but didn't need it because it had been autosaved. He'd also downloaded a demo version of the database software the school used, so the screen felt familiar as he hit the search tab and typed **ALAN ADALE**.

Alan's grin and mighty afro popped up on screen, with a line of file tabs down one side. Robin clicked *Reports* and selected the one that was due to be emailed to parents when term ended in a few days.

After clicking *yes* on a dialogue box that asked if he wanted to edit the report, Robin scrolled down to *Maths*. He changed Alan's grade from a D to a B– and the teacher's comment from *Awkward and disruptive,* to *Tries hard and makes a good contribution.*

Next, Robin opened his own report. Besides being a computer whizz, he liked climbing and archery and his dad had promised him a box of pricey-but-accurate carbon-core arrows if he got a B or better in every subject on his end-of-year report.

Robin was smart, so although he got bored and mucked around a lot, he wasn't surprised to see he'd gotten As for Maths, Computer Studies and Combined Science, and B or B– for everything else except Spanish.

Locksley High's Spanish teacher, Mrs Fabregas, always picked on him (at least in Robin's opinion). One time Robin even wound up in a screaming row, after she sent him to the behaviour unit when at least four other kids were behaving worse than he was.

As Robin changed Mrs Fabregas's C– to the B that would earn him arrows, Alan thumped hard on the door.

'Barclay's coming, with some girl!' he yelled. 'I'm outta here!'

'Are you sure?' Robin shouted back, but Alan had bolted.

Robin frantically changed Mrs Fabregas's *Disrespectful and childish* to *A very enjoyable pupil to teach*, before hitting *save all changes*. Rather than go through a lengthy software shutdown, Robin leaned under the desk and yanked out the power cord.

As he grabbed his backpack off the peeling carpet tiles, Robin could hear a gobby girl outside the door. Mr Barclay was showing her zero sympathy.

'You do not fight in my lunch room!' he was shouting. 'You will wait in my office until I am ready to deal with you.'

'Axel threw potato at me first!' the girl complained. 'Why should I wait in your office? This is a total stitch-up!'

After a quick check to make sure he'd left nothing behind, Robin put one foot on top of the radiator beneath the open window and leaned way out onto the ledge.

As an experienced climber, Robin was confident about swinging his legs off the ledge and sliding down a drainpipe into the school courtyard. But he hadn't expected the pair of wood pigeons perched on brickwork just below.

Startled by Robin's head looming above them, the birds launched into the air. Robin instinctively rolled away from the flapping wings, but lost his grip and slid forward at the same time. His pack caught on the underside of the raised window, but when he reached behind to grab the frame and steady himself the rotting wood crumbled in his hand.

Panic slowed everything down. Robin looked over the ledge at a six-metre head-first plunge into concrete. He grasped for the window again, as the weight of textbooks in his backpack pulled his shiny nylon shorts further over the ledge.

But then – mercifully – he stopped sliding, and felt his sneaker snag on something.

The good news was that the loop of Robin's double-knotted shoelace had caught on the control valve on top of the radiator.

The bad news was that his bodyweight was stretching his sneaker and his heel was slowly sliding out at the back . . .

3. THE BADDEST GIRL AT LOCKSLEY HIGH

I probably should have just worked a bit harder in Spanish class, Robin thought to himself as he dangled.

At worst, he was going to plunge head first into concrete.

At best, Mr Barclay would grab Robin's legs and drag him inside, and he'd *just* be in serious trouble for breaking into the office of the strictest teacher in his school . . .

But something else happened first.

There was a kickabout going on at ground level, and sixteen-year-old Clare Gisborne had just made a clattering tackle. She was the meanest girl in Locksley High and the daughter of Guy Gisborne, the gangster who ran every racket in town.

Clare's flying Nike crunched the other player's knee and an elbow made sure he stayed down. After straddling her crumpled opponent, Clare tapped the battered football into open space and eyed a set of goalposts.

The keeper was rubbish and the only defender between

Clare and the goal had no appetite to tackle after seeing her demolish his teammate.

But as Clare Gisborne teed up a shot in the top left corner, she noticed the stocky little Year Seven kid hanging over a window ledge two storeys up. And while this would have made any decent person freeze in shock, or yell for help, Clare decided it would be hilarious to boot the ball at him as hard as she could.

In his state of panic, Robin saw the leather ball spin in slow motion, making out every scuff and its owner's initials in Sharpie ink. If it hit, Robin would plunge down, but the ball whacked the end of the window ledge with a hollow ping, then spun upward, rattling the glass above Robin's legs.

Clare Gisborne smiled and squinted up into the sun. Tracking the ball as it came down and hoping she could take another shot. But before her foot could connect, Clare got flattened with a hefty two-handed shove.

'Leave my brother,' the lad shouted, breathless from a flat-out sprint across the courtyard.

Everyone called Robin's sixteen-year-old brother Little John. It was an ironic nickname for an absolute giant. But the soccer players gasped because nobody laid hands on Guy Gisborne's daughter.

'Do you know who I am?' Clare roared, as a graze on her cheek filled with blood. 'My dad will feed you to his pigs if he hears about this.'

Clare didn't just talk tough. She sprang up on powerful

legs and dropped into a boxer's stance. Little John worried about Robin and was relieved to see Mr Barclay grab his brother's shorts and yank him inside.

'Come on, you big lump,' Clare growled, swooping and giving John a left-right combo in the gut.

Little John backed up, winded, but holding his hands wide to show he wasn't going to fight back. 'I'm protecting Robin.'

The stinging graze made Clare angry and she launched a roundhouse kick. But John was fast for a big guy and he dodged, leaving Clare's leg whooshing though the air before she stumbled sideways, off balance.

Two floors up, Mr Barclay was overwhelmed, dealing with the angry girl he'd brought from the canteen and struggling to process the fact he'd found a kid dangling out of his office window.

He wished he'd trained as an accountant like his brother as he shouted down, 'Clare Gisborne, John Hood, pack in that nonsense and get out of my sight. Or I will make you both sorry.'

John kept backing away as Clare steadied herself. She shot a nasty glance up at Mr Barclay, then lowered her fists and growled to Little John, 'I won't forget this, John Hood.'

4. JUST YOU WAIT TILL YOUR FATHER GETS HERE

Part of his plastic key had snapped inside the lock, so Robin couldn't claim he'd found the door unlocked. But there was no obvious evidence that he'd hacked the school database, so he still hoped to get away with that.

'I was curious to see if my key would work,' Robin told Mr Barclay, hoping his softest tone and being one of the smallest kids in the school would help his case. 'I saw an article online, about a burglar who broke into houses by photographing the key and using the picture to make a digital file for a 3D printer. I just wanted to see if I could do the same.'

Barclay sat at his desk, with suspicious eyes and a stain from a leaky pen on his shirt pocket.

'Then you came in with that girl, so I went to climb out the window and –'

'You expect me to believe you didn't break in to my office to steal?' Barclay growled, then gave a derisory snort.

'I've been in this office before,' Robin said, glancing around at all the dust and junk. 'What is there to steal?'

Mr Barclay reared up. Robin gripped the sides of his chair, expecting to get a blast for being cheeky. But the teacher had to concede there *was* nothing in the office worth stealing.

'This key you made is ingenious,' Barclay grudgingly admitted. 'You're a clever boy, Robin. I wish you'd channel as much effort into school work as you put into crazy schemes and messing around with Alan Adale.'

'Yes, sir,' Robin said obediently.

'Your father is on his way. We'll discuss your punishments when he arrives.'

Oh God . . . Robin thought.

Robin's dad, Ardagh Hood, was a small man with a big beard, about a billion times less intimidating than Mr Barclay.

But while Robin's dad was never scary, he had a quiet way of looking sad and disappointed when you did something bad. A few hours of sighs and wounded huffing sounds were usually enough to make Robin feel guilty and wish he had the kind of dad who screamed and shouted and got it over with.

'Robin is excluded from school for four days,' Mr Barclay told Ardagh, half an hour later. 'I want to see a two-thousand-word essay about what Robin has done wrong and what he plans to do to improve his behaviour. He'll be on after-school litter patrol for the next half-term. And I've called a locksmith to replace my damaged lock, so you can expect a bill for that too.'

Ardagh nodded and spoke softly. 'Mr Barclay, of course. I'm more than happy to pay for any damage my son has caused.'

'Can I type the essay on a computer?' Robin asked.

Mr Barclay cracked a mean smile. 'By hand. In your best handwriting, and I expect *excellent* spelling and grammar.'

Robin had never written anything half that length before, and felt daunted. He imagined jumping on the desk, defiantly kicking over the stacked files, telling Mr Barclay where to stick his essay and making a heroic leap out the window to freedom.

But he just nodded sourly and said, 'Yes, sir.'

'OK, mister, let's go,' Robin's dad said, sounding so weary it was like he was the one with two thousand words to write.

Robin didn't think Wednesday afternoon could get worse, but somehow it did.

Leaving Mr Barclay's office coincided with the change of lessons. The hallways heaved with students, and they bumped into loads of kids from Robin's year at the bottom of the main stairs. His face turned red as they pulled faces and teased.

'Here's the bad boy!'

'Naughty, naughty, Robina!'

And, 'Fallen out of any windows lately, dumbass?'

Then four alpha-male thugs – the kind of guys you never wanted to stand near in a locker room – started on his dad. Ardagh made an easy target, since his turquoise jelly shoes repaired with plumber's tape, cut-off denim shorts and tie-dyed short-sleeve shirt were a first-degree crime against fashion.

'How come your dad's a hippie, Robin?' one jeered.

A guy shook his head. 'Nah, he's Jesus.'

'Too short for Jesus. He's a garden gnome.'

And rock bottom finally came with white-teethed smiles and mean laughs from Tiffany, Bethany and Stephanie. Three popular girls who looked at Robin the way they'd look at gum stuck to their shoe, on the rare occasions when they deemed it worth looking at him at all.

Ardagh saw his son squirming and placed a hand on the back of his neck.

'Rise above it,' he said airily. 'Always be the better person.'

Dad is a hippie, Robin thought, as he jerked and pushed the hand away.

'Dad, don't touch me,' he snapped angrily. 'Could you be any more embarrassing?'

5. IT'S COMPLICATED NOW WE'RE OLDER

When you're little, it's easy. You see your dad, you run out of school and give him a hug. He tells you he loves you and you don't give a damn who hears it.

Then you're almost thirteen. Sat in the passenger seat of your dad's chugging Ford sedan with a lot of different feelings.

Sorry for what you've done.

Freaked out that you almost got killed.

Cursing the bad luck that meant you got caught.

Mortified that everyone in your class saw your dad wearing shoes held together with sticky tape.

Knowing that your dad is a gentle soul and you crushed him when you told him he was an embarrassment . . .

Robin couldn't look at his dad, so he stared out of the window at his hometown, or what was left of it.

Locksley had been a car-making town. At its peak there were sixty thousand auto workers on good union wages. Rival assembly plants faced each other across the

River Macondo and a car rolled off a production line every twenty-eight seconds. One million cars per year . . .

But the factories moved to sunnier climes, with cheap workers and solar energy. People left to find work. Neighbourhoods emptied, leaving houses worth no more than the electrical cables and copper pipes that could be stripped out and melted for scrap. Locksley High had been built for three thousand kids and now had less than six hundred.

When people and companies left, so did the taxes they paid the City to fix roads, maintain parks, and pay cops, teachers and fire officers. So the town started falling apart, which made more people move away, and then there was even less money . . .

Robin had grown up seeing media reports about Locksley's *spiral of decline*. He saw plenty of evidence as they merged onto a high street of boarded-up shops, empty parking bays, crashed-out addicts and the warped steel frame of a burnt-out Eldridge's department store.

'This isn't the way home,' Robin said, breaching the awkward silence as they stopped at a red light. There were no shoppers wanting to cross, and a postal truck going the other way didn't bother obeying the signal.

'I was at work when Mr Barclay called,' Ardagh answered. 'I have a stop to make, then a class at the library. You can sit at the back and make a start on that essay . . .'

Robin sighed. 'How do I write two *thousand* words?' he moaned. 'Saying sorry is five sentences, tops.'

Ardagh smiled slightly as the light went green. 'Maybe you should have thought of that before you decided to hack Mr Barclay's password and change your report card.'

Robin gulped.

Dad's clever, but how the hell?

'Cat got your tongue?' Ardagh teased. 'I noticed you'd been spending a lot of time looking at hacker forums on the web and wondered why you'd downloaded database software on the computer in the back room.

'I didn't figure it out, until I realised there was nothing worth stealing in Mr Barclay's office, and noticed that the power cable on his PC was pulled out, like someone had switched it off in a hurry.'

'Ahh . . .' Robin said weakly, then asked, 'Why didn't you tell Mr Barclay?'

Ardagh shrugged. 'You might get away with it.'

Robin screwed up his face with frustration. 'Or Barclay might punish me more when he finds out.'

'You're certainly facing a dilemma,' Ardagh agreed. 'Perhaps you could make your two-thousand-word essay into a full confession.'

'You're my dad – tell me what to do!' Robin begged.

'This world is full of sheep,' Ardagh said thoughtfully, as he slowed the car and indicated to turn off. 'I've always set loose boundaries because I want you and John to learn to think for yourselves. But I won't always be around to bail you out.'

Robin squirmed cluelessly in his seat.

'Why don't you message some of your cool friends and see what they think you should do?'

Robin groaned. 'I'm sorry I said you were an embarrassment.'

Ardagh stared at the road, ignoring the apology.

'Dad, *none* of those kids you saw are my friends. I'm the brainy titch. I like archery and computers. I have a rubbish phone and unfashionable trainers. Nobody apart from Alan speaks to me.'

Robin got distracted as they turned off into a parking lot.

They'd reached the liveliest remnant of Locksley High Street, a strip mall, across from the abandoned light-rail terminal where you could once have ridden a tram fifteen stops to the centre of Nottingham.

Hipsta's Drive Thru Donut had mums and tradies seeking caffeine and sugar, and the Curl Up and Dye salon kept busy fixing up elderly ladies who'd starve sooner than cancel their regular hairdo. But they rolled past these and stopped by the aquamarine frontage of Captain Cash.

'What are we here for?' Robin asked. 'You *hate* Captain Cash.'

6. GROUND-FLOOR OPPORTUNITY

Captain Cash was the most successful business to come out of Locksley in the twenty years since the car plants closed. Its colourful stores offered to pay instant cash for stuff like laptops, smartphones and jewellery, or short-term loans at crippling rates of interest.

There were now more than a hundred Captain Cash branches, but it had been founded in a shuttered fried-chicken joint, by three seventeen-year-olds in their final year at Locksley High School.

The first partner was Guy Gisborne. He was the well-brought-up son of a librarian and a dentist, but he'd always fancied himself an outlaw. As a teenager, he'd had several scrapes with the law and served four months in juvenile detention.

Everyone hoped founding a successful business would straighten Guy out. Instead, Gisborne used his share of Captain Cash profits to build a criminal empire, slowly taking over every racket in Locksley and getting most of the town's cash-strapped police force under his thumb.

Marjorie Kovacevic was the second teenaged partner, and the brain to Gisborne's brawn. She turned down places at top universities to run Captain Cash, and six years later masterminded the sale of the business to the multi-billion-dollar King Corporation. With twenty million in her pocket, Marjorie set her mind to politics.

She became Sheriff Marjorie, the youngest person ever elected as Sheriff of Nottingham, which made her boss of an entire county and guardian of the vast Sherwood Forest to the north.

Completing the trio of seventeen-year-olds who didn't listen when adults told them Captain Cash was a stupid idea, was Ardagh Hood. To raise money for the business, he'd worked three after-school jobs, begged his grandfather for a loan and spent an entire summer holiday with Guy and Marjorie, scrubbing grease out of the abandoned chicken shop, patching its leaky roof and hand-painting Captain Cash's first brightly coloured pirate sign.

But Ardagh's vision of an ethical local business that helped hard-up people get a small loan or free up cash by selling stuff they didn't need, was at odds with Marjorie's ruthless quest to squeeze profit out of every customer, and Gisborne using the shop to fence stolen goods and sending thugs to terrorise people who missed a loan payment.

'Your dad would be a very wealthy man if he'd held on

to his share of Captain Cash instead of his principles,' Robin's Auntie Pauline often joked.

Ardagh looked irritated every time his sister mentioned this, but Robin often imagined an alternative life, where they had millions in the bank instead of frozen economy burgers and hand-me-down clothes.

But Robin didn't think about any of that as they stepped inside, because the super-catchy Captain Cash radio jingle was playing on repeat and took over his brain.

Don't take fright when money's tight.
Cos Captain Cash will set you right!

Captain Cash's Locksley branch had long since moved from the former chicken joint where it began into premises ten times the size.

Its illuminated glass cabinets were filled with stuff people can live without when times get tough. Games consoles were stacked like house bricks. Also for sale were pre-loved examples of the smartphone every kid had wanted two years earlier, digital cameras, ping-pong tables, fishing gear, barbecues, wedding dresses and drones.

One entire wall was lined with cool musical instruments like drums and electric guitars that adults buy for themselves, and the ones like flutes and oboes that they nag kids for never practising.

Robin had only been in the store a few times before.

The place was always busy and even at three on a weekday afternoon there were eight people queuing to cash cheques, borrow or sell.

A sturdy man in a farmer's overall at one counter was stressing because they were only offering eighty bucks for his chainsaw.

'Can't you double check?' he begged, flapping a pink Tool Shack invoice in the air. 'This cost over eight hundred bucks. Ninety-six CCs and a diamond chain!'

The weary clerk drummed raspberry-coloured nails on the counter. Her name badge had a cartoon of Captain Cash with a parrot on his shoulder and read, *Hi, I'm Rhongomaiwenua.*

'Sir, we *only* pay the price that comes up on the computer. You've got my queue backed up. So kindly accept my offer, or step aside so I can serve another customer.'

Robin saw the big man's tendons go tight, turning his deep-tanned neck into a lizard collar. At the same time, Ardagh got furious looks as he bypassed the queue.

'Sir!' Rhongomaiwenua snapped at Ardagh.

'I need to see the manager,' Ardagh said gently.

Rhongomaiwenua gave Ardagh the exact look Tiffany, Stephanie and Bethany gave Robin when he got a hundred per cent on a Maths quiz.

'There is no manager here,' Rhongomaiwenua said. 'If you wish to make a complaint you need to call head office in Nottingham.'

'Isla is a friend of mine,' Ardagh insisted. 'Says there's a bunch of computer stuff out back to collect.'

Before Rhongomaiwenua could process this, a sweet-faced woman in a shoulder-padded business suit came out and opened the counter flap.

7. HUNKS OF JUNK TO PUT IN THE TRUNK

'This is my boy Robin,' Ardagh told Isla.

'Out of school early,' Isla noted, as Robin followed his dad behind the counter.

'Long story,' Ardagh sighed.

Robin jumped out of his skin as a huge bang erupted on the counter he'd just stepped through. The giant farmer had raised and smashed down the chainsaw before leaning way over the counter and shouting.

'You people are thieves!' he spat at Rhongomaiwenua. 'Take your offer? You can roll it into a ball and shove it up your . . .'

Robin saw Rhongomaiwenua pressing a red alarm button and two armed security guards shot out of a staff break room.

'Does that happen a lot?' Robin asked, as Isla unlocked a door and took them down a short flight of steps to a store room.

'Only six times a day,' Isla laughed. 'People come in

when they're desperate. They don't like it when we offer less money than they need. But when you've worked here as long as I have, it goes right over your head.'

Robin could hear the security guards and the big farmer in a muffled shouting match as Isla showed them a stack of tatty computers, aged screens, laptops and a black bin-bag stuffed to bursting with cables, mice and keyboards.

'We had a big clear-out of stuff we'll never sell,' Isla explained. 'Some of this works, some doesn't. Take anything you want; the rest will go in the trash.'

Ardagh looked chuffed as he walked around the stack of aged IT gear.

'I'll take as much as I can fit in my car,' he said keenly. 'I teach a computer repair course at the library. We always need gear for the students to tinker with. Anything we clean up and get working is donated to a charity that supplies computers to schools in Congo.'

'Beats going in the trash,' Isla said brightly. 'I'll open up the back door, so you don't have to carry all the stuff through the zoo out front.'

'Ready for some lifting, son?' Ardagh asked.

Robin grabbed a couple of laptops. 'If these work, they're better than the one I've got at home,' he noted.

His dad spoke with unusual sharpness, as Isla found a hand trolley they could use. 'Does today seem like a good day to be asking for a new laptop?'

'I wasn't,' Robin answered defensively.

'I've got to get back to my office to make some calls,' Isla said.

'No problem,' Ardagh said. 'Before you go, did anything happen about the system-security report I wrote?'

Besides his badly paid part-time job retraining unemployed auto workers in IT, Ardagh did freelance work as a white hat, a type of 'good' hacker paid to find weaknesses in security systems by trying to break into them. Robin was fascinated by anything to do with hacking, but shocked that his dad had written a report for Captain Cash.

'I had to get an independent security audit for our insurance company,' Isla explained, lowering her voice so nearby employees couldn't hear. 'Your report told me what I already knew: that our security here is hopeless. But when I called headquarters in Nottingham a month later . . . Nothing. They said there's no budget allocation for IT improvements at this branch.'

Ardagh nodded and spoke so quietly Robin could barely hear. 'When I've done other reports for King Corporation companies, I've had people take me aside and tell me to make sure I *don't* find the very security problems I'm being paid to find. All management cares about is hitting quarterly profit targets and getting their bonus.'

Isla nodded. 'King Corporation made 4.5 billion dollars last year, but my staff have to bring in their own pens, and I don't think there's a single chair in this branch that isn't broken. It's ridiculous . . . But listen, I've *really* got to go make this call. I hope the computers prove useful.'

'They will, for sure,' Ardagh said, as he started loading desktop PCs onto the hand trolley.

8. SENSATIONAL SCENES AT THE LOCAL LIBRARY

Irene led a straight life until she was thirty. She went from high school to a well-paid but mind-numbing assembly-line job that lasted until the car plants closed. Her husband was one of the lucky ones who got transferred to a plant in another town, but after a couple of years he stopped coming home on weekends, then stopped coming home at all.

The second half of Irene's life had been a personal version of Locksley's downward spiral. Drugs, depression and four years in prison after setting up a business selling stolen car parts.

Now Irene was out on parole, and on Wednesday afternoons the tattooed sixty-year-old went to Locksley Library & Learning Centre for Ardagh Hood's Computer & Device Repair course.

'Laptops and phones and stuff are hard to fix because each one is different,' Robin explained, as one of the rescued Captain Cash computers started up on a workbench between himself and Irene. 'But desktops are modular. So, now I've plugged in the display card from that other machine, hopefully . . .'

The screen flickered with a Windows logo, as Ardagh approached.

'Your boy knows his stuff,' Irene told Ardagh cheerfully.

'Our house has been full of computers and junk since Robin was born,' Ardagh explained. 'He's always had a knack with them, though right now he's *supposed* to be sat at the back writing an essay explaining why he can't behave himself at school.'

'Oh dear,' Irene said, giving Robin a cheeky wink as he tapped settings to make the graphics card work at full resolution. 'He's been a great help.'

Robin studied his dad's body language and decided that he didn't really mind him helping with the class.

'So, the machine is running. What are your next steps?' Ardagh asked Irene.

'Ensure the previous owner hasn't left any private data on the system, then run a burn-in program for a few hours to make sure it's stable,' Irene said.

Ardagh gave his pupil a smile. 'You've been paying attention, Irene.'

As Ardagh said this a beautiful woman in too much make-up and designer heels stepped into the IT classroom.

'Ardagh, could we have a little chat?'

Robin had never seen her before, but reckoned it had to

be Mel. She'd been parachuted in to manage Locksley's Library & Learning Centre and his dad often moaned that his youthful boss was inexperienced, incompetent and connected to Guy Gisborne.

As Robin watched Irene check the repaired computer for any personal files, he kept one eye on his dad, who was talking to his boss on the other side of the classroom's glass partition.

The conversation between Ardagh and Mel started off friendly, but after a couple of minutes Robin got worried, seeing his dad slump against the glass with a reddened face and dabbing sweat off his brow.

'Just gonna check on my dad,' Robin told Irene, stepping away from the bench.

As Robin got close enough to the classroom door to hear, Ardagh put a clammy hand against the glass.

'This is insane,' Ardagh was saying. 'Getting rid of me makes no sense.'

'Mr Hood, you know Locksley City runs a competitive re-bidding process for all adult education programmes.'

'How can you teach beginners computing with an online course?' Ardagh said. 'That's like trying to teach soccer to kids who haven't learned to walk yet.'

'Mr Hood, the matter has been decided!'

'I wasn't even consulted,' Ardagh complained. 'I was teaching here when you were at infant school.'

The learning-centre classrooms were set around an indoor courtyard, with seating, leaflet racks and an information desk. It was usually a silent space, so at least twenty people could hear Ardagh and Mel arguing.

'You're set in your ways,' Mel said firmly. 'The new online curriculum will offer a wider range of courses and big cost savings . . .'

Ardagh tutted and shook his head. 'You only got this job because your mother is one of Guy Gisborne's crooked friends.'

Robin worried about his dad losing his job, but felt proud that he was sticking up for himself.

'Mr Hood, your allegation is ludicrous, and I feel threatened by your behaviour,' Mel snapped. 'Please leave the premises and consider yourself suspended pending a disciplinary review.'

Robin noticed the library security officer striding in. A huge fellow in a puffy jacket, who looked like he'd walked into a shop that sold big gold rings and bought the lot.

'Oh, look, another Gisborne crony,' Ardagh said loudly, as he eyed the officer. 'Why bother paying your thugs, when Gisborne can get them cushy jobs on a Locksley City wage? Who'll replace me – a drug runner or a loan shark?'

The guard moved fast, pulling a baton off his belt and wobbling a magazine rack as he charged towards Ardagh.

Robin's stomach flipped as the guard effortlessly bounced his dad against the glass partition and held the tip of his baton against his throat.

'Leave my dad alone,' Robin shouted, acting on instinct as he charged out of the classroom.

The guard eyeballed Ardagh and spoke menacingly. 'You step back in this building, you'll be parting company with teeth. And watch that mouth of yours. Gotta be a fool, disrespecting Mr Gisborne in this town.'

'I'm leaving,' Ardagh said, holding up his hands as Mel made a *kick-him-out* gesture to the guard. 'I just need my bag and keys from the classroom.'

'People who insult Mr Gisborne get to walk home,' the guard grunted, then used his baton to point at a fire exit. 'Shift!'

Robin had been so fixated on his dad, he hadn't noticed the students from the computer repair course coming out behind to watch the action. They made Robin jump as he turned around, then he ducked back into the classroom, grabbing his school bag and his dad's backpack.

'Look after your dad,' Irene told Robin fondly. 'He's one of the good guys.'

A couple of other pupils said something similar.

Robin felt scared and queasy as he sprinted after his dad. He ran awkwardly with the backpack clutched to his chest, and caught up with him in the staff car park at the back of the building. There were no witnesses out here, so the guard had delivered parting gifts with his baton and boot.

Robin found his dad on the ground, clutching his hip and close to tears. He felt as much anger as sympathy towards his father.

'Why don't we load up the car and get out of this crummy town?' Robin growled.

'I'm not going anywhere,' Ardagh said determinedly, as his son offered a hand up. 'Locksley is my home.'

9. GOOD WHOLESOME EXERCISE . . .

Robin was almost the smallest kid in his school, but anyone who tried physical bullying hit trouble. First you had to catch him, and he was fast and could climb like a cat. If you did get Robin cornered, you'd find out that he was extremely strong and might put a judo throw in the mix if you riled him up.

Robin could have made cool-kid status if he'd turned his speed and strength to soccer and spent his limited allowance on sneakers and clothes instead of archery gear and books.

But he was a lone wolf, preferring solo sports and more interested in reading about medieval archery or surfing a hacker forum than hanging with a bunch of boys lying about masterful attainments in video games and how much money their parents were giving them for their birthdays.

Robin's alarm went at 6 a.m. Thursday. Still more eager kid than lazy teenager, he jumped out of bed in the running shirt and grubby shorts he slept in to save time. He crept down from his room in the loft, because Little John was a light sleeper and went nuts if you woke him up.

He grabbed a water bottle from the fridge, which he attached to a Velcro strip on his quiver. This went over his back, along with Robin's most prized possession: an ultra-light carbon-fibre recurve bow for which he'd saved his Christmas money, mowed his auntie's lawn, begged his father – and by some miracle found at forty per cent off when the Nottingham branch of Don's Sports Megastore closed down.

Robin's running shoes were getting a little tight, but he hadn't mentioned it. Partly because he knew they were short of money, but also because he was secretly proud of how trashed they were. A better sign of the training he put in than coloured certificates or medals.

After dramatically leaping the five stairs at the edge of the porch, Robin set off from the grand-but-dilapidated six-bedroom house that had been built by his great-grandma, Agata.

In most towns, it was the place a doctor or lawyer would need a hefty mortgage to buy. But Locksley's grand homes got stripped for scrap, then lasted until bugs chewed through the support beams, or arsonists had some fun.

There had been sixty large houses in Robin's street. Half still stood in some form. None apart from the Hood family pile were officially occupied, though Nottingham University's north campus was within walking distance and a couple had been squatted by groups of students.

Robin set off on a kilometre run to the stop sign at the end of his road. Pushing hard, because exhaustion would blot out worries about his dad losing his job and the two thousand words he had to write for Mr Barclay.

Once his heart was racing, Robin climbed the bars of a rusted gate and dropped into the back garden of Swan House. The copper-domed three-storey home had once been the grandest in the street. It remained in better shape than most, though kids had bricked every window and the basin of the large front pond had been used by skateboarders. But even Locksley's skaters and vandals had mostly moved away. Tags and art were fading, and no new ones had appeared for as long as Robin could remember.

He ran across the puddled basin to an Olympic-sized outdoor pool, now filled only with remnants of burnt tyres and green sludge at the deep end.

One advantage of living amid desolation was being able to come back and find things the way you'd left them. Nobody had been on Swan House's grounds since Robin set up targets at the end of the pool more than six months earlier.

Robin began shooting when his big brother joined an archery club. Little John lost interest when it turned out that a brother four years younger was better than him.

Robin lost interest when he realised that archery club involved standing still, controlling your breathing and shooting at the same static target over and over. One tiny lapse in concentration could mean losing a competition, and the result was that club archery appealed to people whose other hobbies were model trains and craft beer festivals.

But when Robin delved online he found videos of speed archers, who shot rapidly by holding several arrows in their drawing hand, rather than pulling them one at a time from a quiver on their backs.

He YouTubed trick archers, skilled enough to shoot vitamin pills and incoming arrows out of mid-air. Robin's favourite archers combined shooting with parkour and gymnastics, firing arrows while somersaulting or vaulting around a course, hitting targets in rapid succession.

He'd watched their videos hundreds of times, and been surprised how friendly they were when he couldn't figure out how to master certain skills and sent messages asking questions.

There was even a bunch of madmen in Albania who filmed videos where they set arrows on fire and used them to blow stuff up – although they hadn't posted any new videos since the one where Hajar set her boyfriend on fire . . .

Before the invention of gunpowder, archers were the most crucial weapon in battles. Robin read history books full of legends about seemingly impossible archery feats and internet forums where people argued about who the greatest archers were.

Some reckoned it was the Scythians, who massacred thirty thousand Roman legionaries in the Battle of Arbutus. Others vouched for disciplined lines of English longbowmen, or Mongols who were the first to master the art of shooting from horseback.

One story that fascinated Robin was of a Cheyenne tribal chief. Legend said he could shoot one arrow high in the air and fire off ten more before it landed.

Robin wasn't anywhere near ten – not least because his fingers were still too short to hold more than four arrows. But he'd recently mastered a trick where he fired one arrow towards the target at the far end of the pool with a high arcing trajectory, then loaded and shot two more into the centre of a target before the first arrow hit.

Hitting the centre of a target down the length of a swimming pool was something Robin had practised so often, it was almost automatic. But the slower, arcing arrow was vulnerable to a gust of wind so there was always an element of luck.

Robin completed his trick three times successfully, and decided that was an omen.

Yesterday was a nightmare. Today will be awesome.

After retrieving his arrows, Robin took a run and hurdled through a giant window into what had once been a ballroom. Over the past year, he had set up more than fifty targets in the abandoned houses, and while his sprint to the end of the street was always the same, he made the run back an adventure. Taking different routes and shooting his targets from different distances and angles.

After his scare on the ledge the day before, Robin wanted to show himself that he hadn't lost his nerve, so he picked a hazardous route he'd only tried a couple of times before. After a run-up, he made a powerful jump and grasped one of the stair rails on an upper balcony that ran around three sides of the ballroom.

While dangling from the polished rail by the fingertips of one hand, Robin used his strong abs to pull up his legs and hooked one foot between posts. With two firm holds, he swung up, grabbed the railing and flipped over the wooden handrail onto the balcony.

The inside of the wrap-around gallery was lined with empty library shelves, thick with dust and dead bugs. Robin used the shelves as a ladder, then reached up to open an angled roof window. After a rusty squeal as the window swung open, Robin pulled himself through a tight gap and scrambled out onto the sloping roof.

There were missing tiles and one section of the roof was entirely broken away, forcing Robin to cross bare roof-beams. A slight gust made him wobble as he neared Swan House's green copper dome. Scavengers had stripped the easy-to-reach metal around the dome's base, but none had braved going higher to claim the valuable sheets near the top.

This left gaps around the base where the dome's metal

frame was exposed. Robin stuck his head through, peering down three and a half floors into a gloomy mosaicked entrance. If he could find a big climbing rope, maybe someday he'd tie it off and abseil down . . .

But for now, Robin satisfied himself by freeing a loose roof tile and watching as it dropped down and shattered.

10. SIBLINGS HIDE THEIR LOVE FOR EACH OTHER

Robin was suspended from school, so he stayed out longer than usual, doing an extra run through deserted streets. The only other soul he saw was one of the student squatters, jogging in cheetah-print leggings.

'Hey, arrow boy!'

The sun was low but hot and Robin trailed sweaty footprints down the hall as he arrived home. He stumbled into the kitchen with mud-spattered legs, lobbing his empty water bottle in the sink and grabbing another from the fridge.

''Sup?' he said, slightly breathless as he washed his hands.

Ardagh had grapefruit and espresso and a paint-spattered Sony radio tuned to a classical station. Little John overwhelmed a wooden chair at the end of the dining table, eating half a box of cereal from a casserole dish and dressed in his purple Locksley High polo shirt.

'How come Robin's allowed to go out and play if he's grounded?' Little John asked.

Robin knew his brother was stirring, but still took the bait. 'It's not playing. It's *training*.'

'Training is like I do,' John carped. 'At school, with a coach, for an *actual* sport . . .'

'It doesn't have to be,' Robin said, as he grabbed a cereal box and was relieved that Little John had left some. 'I'm fitter than you, faster than you and I'm capable of thinking for myself.'

Rather than intervene, Ardagh turned up his radio and announced, 'There's too much negative energy between you boys! Take some breaths and listen to Mozart.'

'Make Robin shower,' Little John demanded, wafting his hand.

Robin tutted. 'It's a miracle I can get in there, with your epic dumps and the time you spend gelling your stupid hair.'

Ardagh's focus on Mozart was foiled by the station cutting to a commercial.

Don't take fright, when money's tight . . .

'Cos Captain Cash will set you right,' the two boys sang in unison, before laughing.

Robin smiled at his brother, feeling almost fond as he remembered the risk Little John took tackling Clare Gisborne. The brothers loved each other, but did a great job hiding it when there were points to score off their dad.

'Please don't sing that jingle!' Ardagh said gently.

'Robin, your school suspension is supposed to be a punishment,' Ardagh flicked the radio off. 'I don't want you surfing or reading in your room all day. The big shed behind the house needs clearing out, so I can treat the woodworm.'

'Eh?' Robin gawped, as Little John clapped and laughed. 'What about my essay?'

'Nobody's been in that shed in years.' Little John beamed. 'I bet there's dead rats and squirrels! All kinds of nasty stuff . . .'

'You can do the essay over the weekend,' Ardagh said. 'It's a dry forecast today. Pull everything out onto the driveway and hose it or scrub it clean. Then wash down the floors and walls.'

'What's the point cleaning a shed nobody uses?' Robin asked sourly. 'Are you gonna help me, at least?'

Ardagh shook his head. 'I've got two meetings in Nottingham. If I'm not working at the library, I need extra freelance work.'

'No point showering if I'm gonna be crawling around in dirt,' Robin said.

'A commendable decision, Father,' Little John said joyously. 'That boy is out of control. He needs discipline!'

Robin shot up from his Shredded Wheat and yelled. 'Stop winding me up, you massive turd!'

'Stop winding me up,' Little John squeaked, mocking Robin's unbroken voice.

Ardagh eyed his oldest son. 'If you don't cut out the

verbal jabs, *you* can spend the weekend painting the wood with creosote and helping me repair the roof.'

The threat of hard labour shut Little John up.

'Everything's on top of the washer waiting for you,' Ardagh told Robin. 'Key, mop and bucket, hose, dust mask and gloves.'

'I hear it's gonna be *super-hot* today,' Little John said, then tried to look innocent as Robin and his dad scowled at him. 'What, can't I talk about the weather now?'

11. THE BRAVE OFFICERS OF LOCKSLEY P.D.

Robin's room spanned the entire width of the attic. He liked this, because he had archery targets at the far end, and could sit in bed shooting his bow, until his dad yelled because the thud of arrows hitting the target drove him crazy.

Robin felt grumpy as he pulled on a long-sleeved rugby shirt and some old jeans. The whole world was on his back and he was reluctant to admit that it was about ninety-nine per cent his own fault.

He was at the end of his bed pulling his first sock on when he heard a deep growling sound. The traffic out here was light enough for any vehicle to be an object of curiosity, but a jet-engine roar sent Robin scuttling across to look out the attic window.

There were two vehicles approaching the house. The first was a trashed sedan with blue lights and *Locksley Police Department* painted down the side. The second was the source of all the noise, and Robin knew who owned it.

Guy Gisborne had named his customised Mercedes pick-up truck Black Bess. It had a matt-black paint job, enormous spinner wheels, a chromed snorkel exhaust, and a custom-chipped engine good for eight hundred horsepower.

Black Bess broke all kinds of laws, spewing deep grey exhaust, and the mufflers had been removed so it sounded like a race car. But no cop ever dared pull Guy Gisborne over. Nor was any mechanic brave enough to tell him his prized possession had failed an emissions test.

'Dad!' Robin yelled from the top of the stairs.

'I see it,' Ardagh shouted up. 'Stay up in your room. Let me deal with them.'

Ardagh also tried sending John upstairs, and Robin heard his brother stubbornly refusing as the cop car pulled up the driveway, while Gisborne swung aggressively off-road, leaving churned brown tracks across the front lawn.

Two cops in dark blue uniforms waddled to the door.

Ardagh was waiting on the doorstep. 'How may I help you, ladies?'

Robin shuddered, seeing Guy Gisborne step out of the Mercedes, dressed all in black. He'd been Ardagh's boyhood friend, but while most kids grow out of squishing frogs and forcing weaker lads to hand over their lunch money, Gisborne kept getting nastier.

Robin was surprised to see Clare Gisborne jump out

of the passenger side. She was copying her dad's taste for black leather and sunglasses, with a hefty baton swinging off her hip.

'Are you Ardagh Michael Hood?' one of the cops in the doorway asked.

'I am,' Ardagh answered, as Robin crept downstairs to get a better look.

The other cop spoke. 'Mr Hood, following a search of your property, we have discovered four laptop computers that were stolen from the High Street branch of Captain Cash yesterday afternoon. I am therefore placing you under arrest.'

Robin gulped.

The officer took handcuffs from her belt as her partner began reading Ardagh his rights.

'You have the right to remain silent. This means you do not have to say anything, answer any question or make any statement unless you wish to do so, but anything you do say can be used as evidence in the Sheriff's court . . .'

'What search?' Ardagh demanded, as he refused to put his hands out to be cuffed. 'You haven't searched. You just arrived.'

'I can make this as hard as you want it to be,' one officer shouted. 'Give me your damned wrists.'

Robin's heart thumped as he kept creeping down the stairs. He'd heard his dad complaining about Gisborne taking advantage of police cuts to sink his tentacles into Locksley Police Department, but seeing two uniformed officers shamelessly do Gisborne's bidding was still a shock.

'On your knees, Ardagh,' Gisborne demanded, taking a coiled whip off his belt as Ardagh reluctantly accepted the cuffs.

'Leave my dad alone,' John shouted.

'I'll get to you in a minute, Little John,' Gisborne sneered, then eyeballed Ardagh from less than a metre away. 'Knees!' he demanded.

Ardagh defied his boyhood friend, until one of the cops jabbed the back of his thigh with a 50,000-volt stun stick. Clare Gisborne laughed noisily as Ardagh sprawled forward onto his face, groaning and spasming before Gisborne pinned him under his alligator-skin boot.

Robin was now on the landing between the ground and first floor. Four quick arrows would take out the cops and the Gisbornes. Except he'd dumped his archery stuff outside on the porch when he got back in from training . . .

'First your big lump of a son assaults my daughter,' Gisborne began, as he put all his bodyweight behind the heel dug in Ardagh's back. 'Then you dare to stand in the middle of Locksley Learning Centre making nasty allegations about me in front of an audience.'

'You won't get away with this,' Ardagh moaned.

Gisborne laughed, uncoiling his whip. 'Stolen goods worth more than five thousand pounds is a class-C felony, Ardagh. A minimum two-year sentence under Sheriff Marjorie's zero-tolerance sentencing regime. And since your poor wifey dropped dead, I guess I'd better give social services a bell about your boys.'

Robin clutched his fists and stifled a hiss of rage.

You don't make jokes about my dead mum and get away with it.

'But don't worry, Ardagh. I have chums in child services. I'll make sure they're placed in a nice group home on the other side of the forest, so they can't come and visit.'

Ardagh didn't want Gisborne to see him cry and blinked rapidly to stop tears forming in his eyes.

'We could easily drop the boys off at social services,' one of the cops suggested. 'It's no bother.'

Gisborne laughed. 'Get Ardagh on his feet and booked in at the station. I'll deal with these brats, but there'll be extra in your wage packets if he arrives with injuries from his attempted escape . . .'

The cops smiled knowingly at one another as they hauled Ardagh up and marched him out to the battered police cruiser. This left Clare standing back by the front door, while her father closed on Little John.

Being small had taught Robin that mental toughness was as important in any confrontation as size or strength. On paper, Little John was stronger, faster and far bigger than Gisborne. But Gisborne oozed sadistic confidence, while the giant sixteen-year-old was a clammy mess, backing up the staircase, with hands trembling in fear of Gisborne's whip.

'Sit at the kitchen table,' Gisborne ordered, before turning back to his daughter. 'The little one's creeping around upstairs. Go fetch him, so he can witness what happens to people who lay hands on my daughter.'

12. BOXING CHAMP WANTS TO BEAT YOUR ASS . . .

Robin's sixteen-year-old pursuer had brutal speed. The baton swung from her tactical belt as her combat boots stamped up two stairs at a time.

'Come out with your hands up,' Clare demanded. 'The more energy I waste finding you, the harder I'll pound when I get you.'

Robin knew his escape route: the same one he'd used when he drained the ink from two biros into Little John's shampoo bottle.

Robin reached his attic bedroom, then jumped onto his homework desk, reached up to open a roof hatch, then pulled himself up through the hole.

If Clare had looked up when she entered the room, she'd have seen her adversary gently closing the hatch. But she didn't know about Robin's climbing skills and her instinct was to check under the bed, then open Robin's wardrobe.

'I'm a champion boxer,' Clare yelled, as she looked

in the gap between the chest of drawers and the wall. 'I'm gonna hang you upside down and make you my new punchbag.'

Robin had been out on the mossy roof a million times, but quickly discovered that his one socked foot was slippery. After peeling it off, he swung a leg around a brick chimney that ran down the outside wall of the house, to the grand fireplace in the ground-floor drawing room.

He climbed skilfully down vertical brick, suspending himself from strong fingers dug into gaps in the mortar.

After reaching a ledge one floor up, Robin made a two-footed leap onto the roof of the shed his dad had wanted him to spend the day cleaning out. This roof looked fragile, so he spun, dropped and splattered his feet and ankles with mud as he hit the ground. The area was always puddled, because it lay below a broken gutter.

Mud squelched as Robin stumbled towards firmer ground. After a quick look around to ensure there was no sign of Clare, he leaned against the side of the house, thinking up his next move.

13. THE RECYCLING BIN GETS IT

The breakfast dishes were still on the kitchen table as Gisborne lashed out with his whip, shattering the ink-blue vase on top of the refrigerator. Ardagh had been collecting pennies in it for years and now they showered the floor, while shards of blue porcelain flew dangerously.

'Scum like you doesn't touch my daughter,' Gisborne roared, as his boot blasted the recycling bin, spewing milk cartons and flattened cardboard across the floor.

'Robin was hanging off a window ledge,' Little John pleaded, from his seat at the end of the dining table. 'If Clare had hit him with that ball it could have knocked him down and killed him.'

'So what?' Gisborne asked, as he wound the whip back around his hand. 'World's a better place with one less member of your family in it.'

Gisborne picked a jagged shard of blue vase from the floor and closed on Little John with the sharp end. The teen was only wearing the tartan shorts he'd slept in, and his sweaty skin stuck to the chair as he tilted it back.

'This is gonna be a *big* scar,' Gisborne teased sadistically, as the sharp end touched a spot below Little John's earlobe. 'A warning to anyone who thinks about touching my family.'

'She got a tiny graze from some gravel on the courtyard,' Little John said, trying not to tremble because it made the shard push deeper into his cheek.

Gisborne looked around as his daughter arrived in the kitchen doorway, breathing heavily.

'Where's the brat?' Gisborne asked.

Clare's voice was high, like she was properly scared. 'I searched all over. Cupboards, bathrooms, under beds. Robin must have doubled back on me.'

Little John felt relieved, but Gisborne didn't tolerate failure, even from his own daughter.

'He's a scrap of a kid,' he shouted, pounding on the table and making Clare jump.

She stepped closer and gave a pleading look. 'Daddy, I tried *really* hard.'

Gisborne booted the recycling bin again, then wagged his finger furiously in Clare's face.

'If you want to be Daddy's princess and do your hair and wear pretty dresses, you have my blessing,' Gisborne said sharply. 'But if you want to learn the business, you will perform like any other associate and suffer the consequences if you don't. Is that clear?'

Little John almost felt sorry for Clare as he watched

Gisborne signal towards his heavy whip.

Would he hit his own daughter?

'Understood, Daddy . . . I mean, sir,' Clare said, nodding obediently as she backed out and headed for the stairs.

She hoped she'd missed a door. Or maybe there was a loose bath panel someone Robin's size could squeeze behind . . .

Gisborne grabbed the shard off the kitchen table.

'Now, where were we?'

Little John was so scared he thought he might pass out, but his fear of what Gisborne might do if he fought back remained greater than his fear of getting slashed.

At least until the blue glass pricked his skin and drew blood . . .

The spike of pain flipped Little John into a primitive fight-or-flight response. He swung a huge arm, knocking Gisborne sideways. The gangster was surprised by Little John's speed, but quickly regained balance and went for his whip.

'You don't wanna take your punishment?' Gisborne roared, as he lashed out with the whip. 'Then your life just got a hundred times worse.'

The first lash sent a snapping sound through the kitchen and Little John yelped as the whip shredded his T-shirt and left a deep red welt beneath.

Little John stumbled sideways over to the kitchen drainer, grabbing a wooden tray to shield himself, as

Gisborne pulled back for another shot. But as Gisborne swung he felt the whip's handle tear out of his hand.

There was a sharp, hollow thud, and when he looked to see where the whip had gone, he saw its thick leather handle pinned to the door of a kitchen cabinet by an aluminium arrow.

'Hands high, Gisborne,' Robin said, his next shot already loaded and a silver arrow pulled back ready to shoot.

14. OOOF, THAT'S GOTTA HURT

Robin had been squatting outside the front door and reached in to grab his quiver and bow as Clare moved back upstairs.

Then Robin closed in, hoping to surprise Gisborne when he reached the kitchen. But he had to act sooner when Little John threw his punch.

'You haven't got the guts to kill me,' Gisborne taunted, as he stared down Robin's arrow. 'And when you surrender, I'll have you strapped to a door and given a thousand lashes!'

'I don't know if I'm a killer,' Robin admitted, as he lowered his aim. He did a good job keeping fear out of his voice. 'But a shot through your knee will keep you limping for a few months.'

Gisborne smiled, admiring strength even when he was on the wrong end of it.

'So how do I walk out of here, little boy?' he asked, as he cast a wary glance back to see Little John standing passively by the sink, holding his wounded shoulder.

Robin wished he'd thought further than trying to save Little John from getting his face sliced open, as Gisborne daringly took a step closer.

'I need your whip, your wallet and your car keys,' Robin said firmly.

'Where can you go?' Gisborne taunted. 'You can't hide from me.'

'Your people don't control the forest.'

Gisborne laughed noisily. 'A city kid in Sherwood Forest? If the snakes don't get you, the outlaws will.'

Robin backed down the hallway as Gisborne closed in again. His bow felt heavy.

'I'm not debating with you,' Robin said. 'If I let go, this arrow splits your kneecap and comes out the other side.'

Gisborne gestured towards the bottom of the stairs. Robin flinched as he saw a shift in the light above. Clare had made herself known to her father by signalling in a mirror at the bottom of the stairs and now she'd vaulted the stair rail on the first landing.

She crashed down on Robin's back, but not before he'd fired.

'Hell!' Gisborne bawled, doubling over in pain as he crashed backwards into the kitchen table. He was stunned and weakened by the arrow, but still went for his whip. As he lashed out, Little John grabbed a microwave off the kitchen cabinet, snapping the plug out of the socket.

The microwave weighed nothing in Little John's

immense arms. As its door flew open and the glass turntable dropped out, John thrust the end of the microwave into Gisborne's head, making him stagger sideways in a daze.

For all his running, judo and climbing, Robin was helpless under Clare's bulk. A palm thrust to the underside of her chin bought half a second, but Clare had trained with her father and his bodyguards since she was six years old.

She easily flipped Robin onto his belly and snapped him into a brutal chokehold between her thighs.

Using her legs left Clare free to pull a small throwing knife from her tactical belt. Little John made a huge target as he charged fearlessly down the hallway.

Robin's eyes blurred with tears of pain. He was turning blue and shards from the broken vase dug into his chest. But the thought of Little John catching an expertly thrown knife brought out superhuman strength. Robin bucked, freeing his head enough to turn and bite into Clare's trousers.

As Clare yelped, the knife dropped out of her hand. Little John dived, like he was going after a loose ball on a rugby pitch. Robin blacked out for an instant and Little John's bulk crashed into Clare.

Robin's neck crunched and his brother's knee smashing his nose was no less painful for being an accident. Then he wriggled free, gasping and blurry-eyed, as Little John threatened Clare with his clublike fist.

'One move and I'll knock you cold.'

Blinking and bloody-nosed, Robin stumbled into the kitchen to check on Gisborne. Little John's swing with the microwave had knocked him out and he was slumped against a kitchen cabinet, with an arrow sticking out of his . . .

Robin raised hands to his face and gasped. He'd been aiming to shatter Gisborne's kneecap, but Clare's leap had knocked off his aim and his arrow now stuck out of Gisborne's black leather trousers. Deeply embedded in the place where no man wants to get shot.

15. THIS IS A FINE OLD PICKLE

Robin had a bloody nose where Little John caught him with his knee and red drips pelted the kitchen floor as he tied the unconscious Gisborne with his own whip.

Clare was too dazed to resist as John snatched her phone, so she couldn't call for help. Then he stripped off her tactical belt – complete with pepper spray and a big hunting knife – before dragging her into the little toilet under the stairs and barricading the door with a wooden chest, braced against the opposite wall.

'Now what?' John asked, as he faced Robin across the kitchen table.

Little John was three times heavier and four years older than Robin. But he was also a guy who'd spend fifteen minutes staring out of a window deciding whether he needed to wear a coat. So, from picking Dad's birthday card to figuring out what to do when the town's number-one gangster was tied up in the kitchen, there was only ever going to be a decision if Robin made it.

'We're dead meat if we stay here,' Robin said, his voice nasal because his head was tilted to stop the bleeding. 'Gisborne's people will soon realise he's missing.'

Little John nodded. 'But where do we go? Aunt Pauline's?'

Robin tutted. 'Two whole streets away? And the first place they'll look.'

'Where, then?'

'Sherwood Forest.'

John looked appalled. 'It's full of snakes and outlaws,' he blurted. 'Gisborne said we won't last five minutes.'

Robin tutted. 'Stay in Locksley until Gisborne's goons find you, if you like. I'm packing gear and hiding in the forest.'

'We could get a train or bus to the capital,' John suggested. 'You can vanish in a big city as easily as the woods.'

'The only bus from here goes to Nottingham, a town crawling with Gisborne's thugs and Sheriff Marjorie's people. From Nottingham there's a train south every few hours, but you can bet Gisborne will have spies looking out for us. And if you're thinking of a taxi, guess what?'

Little John sighed. 'Every taxi driver in town pays off Gisborne to keep their job.'

'Pack a bag, *quickly*,' Robin urged, as he reached into Gisborne's leather coat and dug out his phone and the keys to his truck.

'Gisborne loves that truck,' John said.

'One advantage of shooting him in the nads and knocking him out is that it's impossible to make Gisborne any angrier,' Robin pointed out, almost managing a smirk. 'And Dad's car takes five minutes to warm up.'

'If it starts at all,' Little John agreed. 'But I only had three driving lessons with Dad during the Easter holidays.'

'The forest isn't far,' Robin said. 'And there's never any traffic out that way.'

Clare was pounding on the door under the stairs and Gisborne had started coming around.

'Go pack,' Robin ordered. 'Keep it light. Once we get to Sherwood we'll be moving on foot.'

After quickly double-checking the knots he'd used on Gisborne, Robin followed his brother upstairs.

The bottom half of Robin's trousers was covered in flaking mud, so he switched to a pair of trackies. He dug his life savings of forty-three pounds from under a loose floorboard, and decided it was worth carrying the weight of his laptop because all his hacker and archery contacts were saved on there, and apart from his bow it was the only thing he owned that might be worth a few pounds.

Robin topped off his bag with a waterproof jacket, a fleece, dry socks, a water bottle, chocolate ginger biscuits and underwear.

The pack was heavier than he'd have liked, and he'd have to carry his crossbow and quiver as well.

After stopping in a first-floor bathroom to grab

a toothbrush, sunscreen and a few other bits, Robin crossed to Little John's room.

The sixteen-year-old had found a large backpack and pulled piles of stuff out of his drawers, but was paralysed deciding what to put inside.

'Gisborne's people will kill us for sure,' Little John blurted, almost tearful. 'And they've got Dad.'

Part of Robin wanted to yell at his brother to focus, but anger only made Little John worse when he got into a state. So Robin took over and started stuffing the bag. As he headed out of Little John's room, Robin remembered he hadn't packed a torch and raced back to the attic.

Downstairs, Gisborne was conscious and moaning into the dishcloth Robin had used as a gag. More alarmingly, Clare had taken the heavy porcelain lid off the toilet cistern and was smashing it against the under-stair door.

Robin handed Gisborne's keys to Little John as they scrambled out of the front door.

'What if I crash?' John asked.

'Try not to,' Robin suggested, as they reached Gisborne's wheels.

16. IF YOU GO DOWN TO THE WOODS TODAY

Black Bess's interior had hand-stitched Italian leather seats with GG embroidered on the headrests and more loudspeakers than a heavy metal concert.

Little John pushed the big red *start* button and the huge engine set the whole cab shaking.

'What do I do?' he shouted over the clatter.

It was frustrating dealing with John when he got in a panic. Robin wondered if it might have been better to run. But they were five kilometres from the forest, they were carrying a lot of stuff, and Little John didn't exactly have a distance-runner's build.

'The controls are the same as Dad's car,' Robin soothed, as the race-tuned engine revved and choking sooty plumes engulfed the truck.

He pointed at the transmission. 'Try putting it in drive,' he suggested. Robin was pinned to his seat as Black Bess shot across the front lawn on an alarming trajectory, straight towards the house.

'Steer!' he yelled.

The black Mercedes clattered through their dead grandmother's rose bushes and flattened the headstones of Barry the tortoise and two beloved Hood family dogs.

'It's got more grunt than Dad's wagon,' John observed.

They bounced on towards the double garage of the neighbouring house and John slowed down to turn, just as Clare ran out onto the lawn. She hadn't looked, assuming her dad's car would be escaping rather than doing a bumpy circle around the front lawn.

Only Little John's foot on the brake and a frantic dive into prickly rose bushes stopped Clare from becoming a gooey splat on Black Bess's formidable front bull bars. Robin feared his nose would start bleeding again as he thumped the dashboard.

'The road!' he demanded. 'Aim for the road!

John sped up and the front wheels finally hit the street.

Robin realised he'd made a mistake as he looked backwards through the rear window. 'Clare's going back inside. We took their phones, but I should have ripped the landline out of the wall.'

'Gisborne's got flunkeys all over town,' John said warily, as he took a left at the end of the road. 'And this car doesn't exactly blend into its surroundings.'

'We'll bail as soon as we get into the forest,' Robin said, as they drove a straight road with farmland on either side. 'It's ten minutes unless we hit traffic.'

There was one lane in each direction, so John had to

pull out to overtake a tractor dragging a trailer stacked with hay bales. As he came back into his lane, they heard a siren, but the oncoming vehicle was hidden by the crest of a hill.

'That's not good,' John said.

'It's no use turning away from the forest,' Robin said nervously. 'Keep your head. Speed up if you're comfortable.'

The engine belched as John took the truck up to 80 kmh, and the tractor receded in his mirror.

An empty yellow school bus, heading to its first morning pick-up, came the other way and Robin felt monster relief as a wailing ambulance – not a cop car – emerged through the haze of low sun.

'Going to our house, for Gisborne?' John wondered.

'If it is, Locksley P.D. won't be far behind.'

Sherwood Forest's vast canopy stretched out below as they crested a hill. It was the largest forest in the land, a hilly green mass extending north for seventy kilometres, and stretching four hundred and fifty from east to west, in a great belt from the waterfalls at Lake Elizabeth to the swampy Eastern Delta.

Black Bess drove downhill fast and noisy, coming to a rusted blue sign before a fork in the road. To the left was Route 24, a twelve-lane asphalt scar that cut Sherwood Forest in two. John went right, forced to slow by gaping potholes and reddish silt deposited by spring floods.

There were huge signs on each side of the road. The

first was green, with two smiling cartoon trees and King Corp's golden crown logo, which angry folks had shot through with bullet holes.

WELCOME TO SHERWOOD FOREST
PART OF THE LOCKSLEY SPECIAL ENTERPRISE ZONE
A CARING PUBLIC-PRIVATE PARTNERSHIP MANAGED BY THE KING CORPORATION

On the other side a mangled yellow warning sign had been left at a strange angle after an encounter with a drunk driver:

NO REFUELLING STOP FOR 104KM
DANGER OF FLASH FLOOD
DANGER OF WILD ANIMALS
DANGER OF BANDITS
HAVE A NICE DAY

John didn't fancy any of that as he rounded a sharp corner, then had to slam on the brakes.

Neon-orange Forest Ranger trucks were parked one on either side of the road. Between them ran a metal stinger strip, whose jagged metal barbs would shred the tyres of any vehicle that went over it.

'Might be a routine check,' Robin said. 'Rangers do search vehicles for criminals and stuff.'

But there was nothing routine about the brown-uniformed Ranger who ran out, waving her arms and making *halt* gestures towards the black truck.

'Turn off your engine,' her lieutenant ordered through a bullhorn, as John squealed to a stop thirty metres shy of the roadblock. 'Place your hands on the dashboard.'

So far, Little John's entire driving experience had been forward. As he looked at the transmission, trying to find reverse, more Rangers jogged out of the trees and trapped them by springing a second stinger strip in the road behind.

'We're screwed!' John said, pounding on the steering wheel.

'We've got massive bull bars on the front and a *lot* of power,' Robin said, pointing at the left-side Ranger truck, which had open scrubland behind it. 'Smash it.'

John gawped. 'Seriously?'

'What choice have we got?' Robin said. 'We're as good as dead if they catch us.'

Robin buried his head, fearing Rangers' bullets as John practically stamped the accelerator pedal through the floor.

17. A LOVELY MORNING STROLL

Black Bess spewed black exhaust and black rubber smoke from huge black tyres.

She was the same type of Mercedes truck that Forest Rangers used, but with Gisborne's modifications this was like comparing a regular person with a pro bodybuilder.

Beige-uniformed Rangers scattered, terrified by Black Bess's roar. Her huge front wheels swerved off-road and reared into the parked Rangers' truck. Glass smashed as the front bull bars ripped the doors and rear fender off the Rangers' Mercedes, before flipping it on its side.

Three of Black Bess's wheels were off the ground and Robin thought they were wedged. But one wheel dug in, flinging up huge clods of dirt. After a sudden jerk and a sharp bang, they were clear.

One forward-thinking Ranger had sprinted down the road with a third stinger strip, but she could only deploy it a fraction after Black Bess drove past.

Leafy darkness enveloped the Mercedes as it blasted under the forest canopy.

'That was no fun,' Robin gasped, as he looked back and saw a bullet hole in the rear screen. It couldn't have missed his head by more than twenty centimetres, but with all the noise and chaos, he hadn't noticed when it hit.

The stinger strips were spring-loaded, so they could rapidly eject in front of an oncoming vehicle. But they had to be dragged out of the road by hand, and the tyre-shredding barbs tended to catch in cracks, or slice the hands of officers who weren't careful.

While the Rangers' surviving truck got held up behind their own stinger strips, John accelerated to seventy. But as he got into a groove, slinging Black Bess into winding forest curves, the dashboard screens turned to blank grey and John felt power drain from the engine.

'What did you do?' Robin asked, as the engine cut, leaving sounds of gravel pelting the car's undertray.

'Don't blame me,' John said, baffled as he glanced at the transmission stick and jiggled the key to restart the engine.

Robin wondered if an unseen Ranger's bullet had damaged something, but the mystery was solved when he looked at the navigation screen:

Satellite Immobiliser – Activated

'It's a tracking system,' Robin announced. 'I've seen the TV ad. If you report your car stolen, the system broadcasts a kill code.'

As they rolled to a halt on the narrow forest road, the boys could hear the Ranger truck closing on them. But the full horror dawned when Robin tried his door.

'It's locked us in,' he yelled.

As John furiously pulled at the door handle, Robin clicked off his belt and scrambled behind his seat. The bullet through the back windscreen had partially torn the glass from its frame. It was laminated safety glass and Robin realised the shattered screen would peel off, like the ring-pull on tinned soup.

John had a job squeezing between the front seats, as Robin threw out two backpacks and his bow. The Rangers' truck squealed to a halt as the brothers jumped from the flatbed behind the cab and charged for the trees.

After half a minute forging through dense branches, Robin stopped and shushed John.

'I can't hear them,' he whispered.

The forest canopy was sixty metres up, and little light reached the ground.

'I've heard King Corp pays Forest Rangers minimum wage and that outlaws hunt them for sport,' John said quietly. 'I guess they don't like venturing off the main road.'

Robin smiled and took a moment to enjoy the forest's fresh, earthy air.

'Finally, some luck,' he told Little John, then tripped on

a tree stump hidden in shadows and stumbled forward.

Robin felt terror, realising there was nothing below his feet.

He felt pain as he got lashed by bushes growing from the ravine's near-vertical wall.

Finally, he felt nothing at all, as he stopped tumbling twenty metres below where he'd started and thumped head first into a rock.

18. LADIES IN BALACLAVAS

'Robin?' Little John shouted, holding on to a tree trunk and peering down the steep embankment.

Except he didn't fully shout because he was afraid the Rangers would hear.

It sounded like water ran at the bottom of the ravine, but it was gloomy, and beyond branches flattened by the start of Robin's tumble, all John saw were dense green tangles.

He imagined Robin crawling up with a wry smile, saying, *Phew, that was close.*

Or, failing that, a shout that would confirm Robin was conscious and give some clue where he was. But there was just the eerie music of bugs and birds in the canopy, then a chattering sound as a yellow-striped lizard shot across a branch in front of his face.

Little John jumped back, feeling trapped and gulping air. A bird shrieked noisily, and he grasped the branches tighter, panicked and imagining himself falling.

'Robin?' he half shouted again. 'You'd better not be pranking me.'

I wish you were pranking me . . .

As hope of Robin reappearing faded, John backed away and looked skywards. Decisions always did his brain in. This one was huge, and his brother might die if he got it wrong.

He considered clambering down, but the slope was close to vertical. He felt an itch in his back and glanced around. There was a fanged beetle as big as his thumb stuck to his shirt. Its front claws were moving but the rear had been squished when his backpack shifted, and snot-coloured goo oozed through its cracked shell.

'Gross,' John said, flicking it away then setting off back to the road.

'Rangers!' John yelled, fearfully and at full blast. 'Can anyone hear me?'

He couldn't exactly retrace his steps through dense undergrowth, but the sun gave some sense of direction. He scrambled out onto the dirt road, sixty metres behind Black Bess. He held his hands in the air as he stumbled towards three shadowy figures around the car.

'Don't shoot!' he shouted. 'I surrender. My brother needs help!'

As Little John got closer he sensed something wrong. There was no sign of the bright orange Ranger trucks and the three female figures wore jeans and knitted balaclavas, not tan-coloured Ranger uniform . . .

As the women turned away from Black Bess towards John's shout, someone stepped out from the bushes alongside him.

'Stop right there,' she demanded.

She was short and stocky, dressed in mud-caked jeans, beat-up body armour and a knitted balaclava the colour of English mustard. There was a ratcheting sound as she released the safety on an old-fashioned Thompson machine gun with a huge drum-shaped magazine.

'On your knees, hands on head.'

Little John pointed into the trees as his knees hit the dirt.

'My little brother fell down a ravine. He could be hurt.'

Two more women in boots and body armour strode across from Black Bess.

'Do you have the key to that car?' the one in the lead asked.

'It's immobilised,' John said, as he pointed again. 'My brother –'

'Hands on head!' the one with the machine gun repeated. 'Are you deaf?'

'You took *that* car for a joyride?' a tall woman with a purple balaclava said, before snorting. 'Do you know who it belongs to?'

Little John nodded.

The women swapped glances and laughed warily.

'You stole Guy Gisborne's wheels?' the one pointing the machine gun said. 'And now you're stuck way out here . . .'

'Up the creek without a paddle,' the tall purple balaclava teased, as she stepped closer.

An older woman, who'd stayed back trying to get Black Bess running, arrived on the scene and took charge. She had a bright yellow stun gun on her belt and straggly grey hair spilled from the back of her balaclava.

'Car's proper dead,' she announced. 'The alloys are worth money, but no scrap dealer will touch parts stripped from Gisborne's rig.'

'Please, my brother,' Little John pleaded. 'He could be badly hurt.'

The one with the machine gun laughed. 'Better dead out here than what'll happen when Gisborne finds you.'

Little John felt tears welling. 'Robin's only twelve.'

He hoped he'd stirred some motherly instinct as the tall one and the old one glanced at each other.

'Rangers will be back with a tow truck, and this is Brigands' territory,' the tall one said coldly. 'We need to ship out.'

'What about this big lump?' the one with the gun asked.

'He comes with,' the older woman said decisively. 'I'll bet Gisborne's put a fat bounty on his head already.'

19. THE BEAUTIFUL QUALITIES OF MARION MAID

Robin's lids felt gluey, so he assumed he'd been sleeping for some time. One nostril was wedged with clotted blood. He felt like there was an axe embedded in the back of his skull and his arms and chest had dozens of grazes and a deeper wound with four stitches below his nipple.

He remembered crashing through branches into the ravine, but nothing after. Now he breathed dead indoor air, tinged with pee and disinfectant.

Robin jerked up, fearing Rangers had hauled him out of the ravine and locked him in one of the Sheriff's cells. He could almost feel Gisborne's whip on his back, but then realised there was nothing institutional about his hand-sewn patchwork blanket. Plus, there was a large fire door wedged open to let in a breeze and a *Get Well Soon* graffiti mural on the far wall.

'So, you lived,' a girl said sarcastically, as she approached.

Robin wondered if he was dreaming, because his

vision was blurred and there was something unnervingly beautiful about her.

She looked about Robin's age and moved with a slight limp. She wore an unzipped hoodie with fraying cuffs, over a summer dress patterned with yellow roses. Huge swimming-pool-blue eyes contrasted with a split lower lip and grimy hands with dark crescents under chipped nails.

'Where am I?' Robin asked, pain shooting through his head as he shifted to get comfortable.

The room was filled with light from a low sun, and he felt sure it was morning.

'You're safe,' the girl soothed, combing her fingers through her tangled hair as she settled in the orange bucket-chair beside the bed. 'This is our free clinic. We're shabby, broke, and our only doctor is eighty-three years old. But we do our best.'

Now he'd sat up properly, Robin could see the empty bed next to him, and an elderly man attached to a drip by the far wall.

'How'd I get here?' Robin asked uncertainly.

'Why were you in the forest?' the girl asked.

'Had to run,' Robin said, deciding to keep things vague, because he didn't know where he was, and Gisborne had friends everywhere. 'My dad got busted on some trumped-up theft charge, and the cops were after me too.'

'It's a big forest. You're lucky we found you.'

'Where was I?' Robin asked.

'I was checking fish traps along a stream with my cousin

Freya,' the girl explained. 'It was starting to get dark, but as we were about to head home I noticed blood swirling in the water. I tracked it back, expecting a wounded deer or badger. You were unconscious but breathing.'

The girl pulled out her phone and showed Robin a picture she'd taken when she found him.

His legs had wound up in a shallow pool. The top of his backpack and the rocks around were stained dark red, and arrows had spilled out of his quiver.

'That's a lot of blood,' Robin said queasily. 'What about my brother?'

The girl shook her head. 'You were alone.'

Robin's looked worried. 'Seriously? No sign of him?'

The angst sharpened his mind. It was morning when he fell, and the girl said it was getting dark when she found him. Anything could have happened to Little John in the hours between. From being captured by Rangers to death in the ravine.

'I closed the big cut on your head with superglue and knotted together hair from either side to keep it sealed,' the girl continued.

Robin's eyebrows shot up. 'Superglue!'

'Always keep a tube in my medical pouch,' she explained. 'You need first-aid skills if you're planning to survive in Sherwood Forest.'

Robin nodded. 'That and a lot of other things.'

'Luckily you're not so big. Freya chucked you over her shoulder and we ran here, to the clinic.'

Robin's tongue felt like a scouring pad. 'Can I drink?' he croaked.

He fretted about Little John as the girl found a water jug and a stack of disposable cups on a trolley by the open doors. Her right leg was noticeably thinner than the left and there was an operation scar down the length of her calf.

'I was born with a club foot,' she explained, looking ashamed as she handed Robin the flimsy cup. 'They operated to even my legs up when I was six, but I've gone back to being a freak as I've grown. One foot twisted and three sizes smaller than the other . . .'

Robin felt embarrassed that she'd caught him staring.

'You're not a freak,' he said, then hid his face by gulping water.

Sometimes things are beautiful because they're perfect and sometimes they're beautiful because they're not. Robin's eyes blurred less now he'd blinked, but he was still fascinated by the girl's amazing eyes, squashed nose and grubby hands. He desperately sought the right thing to say.

Not something creepy like, *You're pretty.*

Not something patronising like, *I hardly noticed your wonky leg . . .*

But inspiration failed to strike, and Robin wound up blurting, 'I'm really short, so . . .'

More intelligently he added, 'You saved my life and I don't know your name.'

'Marion Maid,' she said, smirking at Robin's unease as he crushed his empty water cup.

'I'm Robin Hood.'

Marion nodded. 'When you got here, Dr Gladys made me check your wallet, in case you had a medical alert card.'

'You saw that goofy photo on my school ID?' Robin asked self-consciously.

Marion nodded and laughed. 'Getting ink on your cheek was a nice touch . . .'

Robin glanced up and was surprised to see a cluster of mirrored disco-balls on the ceiling and a suspended sign pointing to *Kids' Department* and *Fitting Rooms*.

He gave Marion a baffled look and asked, 'Where exactly am I?'

20. DELUXE SHOPPING EXPERIENCE

'This used to be a big-ass shopping mall,' Marion answered, then spoke in a deeper, mocking tone, like she was commentating on a TV documentary.

'The Sherwood Designer Outlets was once the region's premier shopping destination, with bargain hunters packing out one hundred and seventy retail units.'

Robin smiled as Marion reverted to her normal voice. 'People from Locksley stopped buying trendy kicks and designer handbags after the car plants closed. And Chinese tourists stopped coming when forest bandits started robbing tour buses at gunpoint. So now us Forest People use the abandoned mall for shelter.'

'So you're a bandit?' Robin said.

Marion narrowed her eyes and sounded narked. 'Forest People aren't *all* criminals,' she growled. 'Despite what TV pundits and Sheriff Marjorie would have you believe.'

'Sorry. I didn't mean . . .'

'My mum and auntie came to Sherwood as hunt sabs before I was born.'

'What's that?' Robin asked.

'Hunt saboteurs,' Marion explained. 'Sheriff Marjorie has stuffed the forest around Sherwood Castle with exotic animals, and rich people pay a fortune to shoot them for their *supposed* sport. Hunt sabs do everything possible to disrupt hunting parties. Drums and sirens to scare the animals off. They release animals bred for hunting from cages, drop paint bombs on the hunters and chop down trees to block paths.'

'Do you do that stuff?' Robin asked.

Marion did a *yes-no* gesture. 'I was born in the forest. I'd obviously like to stop hunting, but Sherwood's my home and I care about a lot of other stuff too. People are in the forest for a million different reasons.

'There are people like you, on the run from cops. On the lunatic fringe, you've got religious cults and anarchists. There are isolationists who believe the government is out to get them and ecologists who want to be at one with nature. There are campaigners like my mum and charity workers like Dr Gladys, who set up this free clinic.

'Obviously there are *some* criminals and bandits. But by far the biggest group in Sherwood Forest are refugees and migrants. Thousands of people who came to this country to escape wars and famines and stuff.'

As Marion finished her explanation, a man strode purposefully into the room. He had a Union Jack bandana tied around his head. His age was hard to read, with youngish dark skin and a trim physique, but brown peg teeth suggesting either a hard life or too much candy.

'Robin woke up,' Marion told the man brightly, as he approached. Then she looked at Robin. 'This is Will Scarlock. He's the boss of Designer Outlets.'

'Because nobody else wants the hassle,' Will added as he reached over the bed to shake Robin's hand.

'I've heard that name *Scarlock* somewhere,' Robin mused, as Will inspected his head wound.

'Marion did a grand job gluing your big cut,' Will said, ignoring Robin's question.

'You probably saw Will's name in the news,' Marion said proudly. 'Sheriff Marjorie has a two-hundred-and-fifty-thousand-pound bounty on his head and the Japanese fisheries minister called him a *terrorist menace* after he blew up a whaleboat.'

'We made sure nobody was on board,' Will emphasised, as he glanced at his watch, then at Marion. 'I've had Freya on the radio. Our crew successfully robbed the truckload of silver cutlery, but Castle Guards shot them up as they got away. At least three are going to need treatment and there's only one spare bed in the clinic.'

Robin was intrigued by the tale of a robbery, but it didn't sit with Marion's claim that her people weren't bandits . . .

'Looks like you've got your marching orders,' Marion told Robin.

'You've lost a lot of the red stuff, so go easy and don't be surprised if you're light-headed when you start moving around,' Will cautioned. 'Dr Gladys said you're fine, so Marion will take you to her family den and her mums will keep a good eye on you.'

'Feel up to walking?' Marion asked. 'Or would His Majesty like a wheelchair?'

21. REDISTRIBUTION OF WEALTH

Robin didn't need a wheelchair, but the back of his head was painful, and he was way off full strength as he followed Marion out of the twelve-bed clinic. In one direction lay the unlit arcade that ran down the centre of the mall, in the other a set of plywood steps led to a rectangular hole cut in the mall roof.

'I can give you a tour up top,' Marion offered, pointing towards sun blazing through the hole. 'Or you can rest in our den. My three little brothers are brats, but they'll clear out if I threaten to thump them.'

Robin had ten aches and six pains, but he was curious about his surroundings and knew he'd get crazy bored doing nothing all day.

'The air-con's dead and our drains get stinky when it hasn't rained,' Marion explained, as she walked up the steps behind Robin, with his pack, quiver and a slightly scraped bow slung over her shoulders, 'so most action happens up on the roof.'

Robin felt overwhelmed by chatter and bustle as his eyes adjusted to bright sunlight on a flat roof that stretched at least a hundred metres in every direction.

Will's eighteen-year-old son, Sam Scarlock, stood over a giant wok tossing peppers, mushrooms and new-laid eggs. Little kids chased around, and half a dozen people sat on brightly coloured prayer mats, sharing coffee from a dented steel pot.

Further off, the flat roof had an informal market selling homewares and groceries; huge rusting satellite dishes; male and female shower blocks; a hydroponic vegetable garden; solar panels; three giant chicken coops and a troublingly frail three-storey observation tower, whose lookouts had powerful binoculars and sniper rifles.

'I had no idea bandi— I mean Forest People, were so organised,' Robin said, which made Marion laugh.

'It's not *that* organised, but Will mostly keeps water flowing, puts food on the table for everyone and generates enough electricity for essential services, like light and Netflix . . .'

Robin made a sun visor with his hand, to see what lay beyond the roof.

In the fifteen years since Sherwood Designer Outlets closed, the forest had eaten into the vast open-air parking lots. Prickly purple-flowered bushes grew from every crack in the tarmac, and in places trees had punched through, some up to ten metres tall.

'Marion-yon-yon!' a woman said playfully as she jogged

up and gave Marion a friendly thump on the shoulder.

She was striking and heavily tattooed, and her deodorant had been overwhelmed by a night of exertion in Sherwood Forest. She carried a towel and a washbag and had bloodstained bandage wound around one well-developed bicep.

'Robin, this is Azeem,' Marion said. 'Just back from stealing silver.'

'Pleasure,' Azeem said, as she fist-bumped Robin.

'How was the raid?' Marion asked. 'Anyone hurt bad?'

'Did the job but it got rough,' Azeem said, shaking her head. 'You can't run fast with thirty kilos of silver cutlery rattling around in your pack and Castle Guards on your tail, shooting up trees.'

Marion explained for Robin's benefit. 'You can't get a straight shot at a target in dense forest, so Castle Guards aim their machine guns into the canopy and shatter tree trunks.'

'A wooden shard through an artery is as deadly as a bullet,' Azeem added, as she tapped her bandaged arm. 'My splinter was no bigger than a cotton bud, but we had to stretcher one lad who got a big spear through his body armour.'

'Are Castle Guards the same as Rangers?' Robin asked.

'Heck no!' Marion said angrily. 'Rangers are locals. They patrol forest roads, pick up broken-down cars, deal with poachers, floods and forest fires.'

'Rangers will bust you if they catch you doing something illegal,' Azeem said. 'But they don't rough you up.'

'Castle Guards are ruthless,' Marion continued. 'They're Sheriff Marjorie's personal stormtroopers. Ex-military, hard as granite. They're supposed to be private security guards protecting Sherwood Castle and the surrounding estate, but they go *way* beyond that.'

Robin didn't want to rile people who'd saved his life, but felt he had to ask the awkward question.

'So, you're *not* bandits . . . But you robbed a truck filled with silver cutlery and got shot at by Castle Guards?'

Marion glared, but Azeem cracked up laughing.

'Sheriff Marjorie would call us bandits, but that's not how we see ourselves,' Azeem explained. 'Real bandits are in it for themselves. They'd rob another forest person's food, sell drugs, kidnap refugees to work in sweatshops and generally prey on the weak. Our crew just takes what we need. We train to fight, but only use violence if we have to and we only steal from the big fish, like Sheriff Marjorie and King Corporation.'

'Everything they have comes from ripping off ordinary people in the first place,' Marion added, before Azeem continued.

'We were tipped off by a source who works at Sherwood Castle. A huge summer hunt is being organised. The source told us Sheriff Marjorie spent a hundred thousand pounds on a solid-silver cutlery service for the castle's banqueting room. Last night, we laid out stinger strips in front of the delivery truck, tied up the driver and robbed it.

'We'll melt and sell the silver, but that money will go in a flash. Will's wife Emma distributes food parcels, blankets and maps for refugees whose boats wash up in the Eastern Delta. The mall plumbing needs an eight-thousand-pound overhaul to stop us choking on the smell of drains. We've also had thieves sneaking into the mall at night stealing, so Will wants night-vision goggles for our security patrols.'

'Don't forget the cost of running the clinic,' Marion said. 'Where you just spent the night in a free bed, had a three-hundred-quid plasma infusion to replace the blood you lost and left with sixty pounds' worth of antibiotic pills, antiseptic cream and replacement dressings.'

'I get it,' Robin said, wishing he'd phrased the bandit question more delicately. 'You steal from the rich and give to the poor . . .'

22. THE *LOCKSLEY GAZETTE* IS A BIASED RAG

'Gotta wash away my stink!' Azeem said, waving her towel like a flag as she backed away. 'Fab to meet you, Robin.'

After a few steps Azeem stopped by a lively group cooking flatbreads on a hotplate and began speaking fluently in Arabic. The only word Robin made out was his own name.

'I think Azeem is asking them to give you food,' Marion explained. 'Are you hungry?'

Pain and worry made it hard to gauge his appetite, but Robin hadn't eaten since breakfast the previous morning and figured he ought to try.

As they stepped onto a lavish Persian carpet, an elderly woman drizzled honey on a square of her just-baked flatbread and passed it to Robin. The warm flaky dough and melting honey made him smile as he bit into it.

'*So* good!' Robin said, trying not to get honey on his fingers as he took a huge second mouthful.

'It's a Moroccan bread called *m'smen*,' Marion said, as she got a slice for herself. 'I could live off this stuff. Especially when it's still hot.'

The baker seemed pleased with Robin's reaction, but in the background three women and a boy aged about nine were frantically chattering in Arabic. Robin kept hearing his name, but was baffled as the boy pointed at his bow, which was over Marion's shoulder because of his weakened state.

The slender boy stepped in front of Robin and nodded. His face was young, though he was almost Robin's height. He looked down at the carpet and spoke nervous English, his pronunciation excellent, but each word requiring brow-furrowing concentration.

'My lady the grandmother wants to ask,' the boy began, as he pointed at a woman sitting on the carpet, 'are you Robin Hood, who used a bow to shoot Guy Gisborne in his . . .'

The boy didn't know the English word, so he looked down and made a pained expression and a cupping gesture between his legs.

Azeem still hadn't gone for her shower and shrieked when realisation hit.

'You're that kid who shot Guy Gisborne in the grapes!' she blurted, pointing at Robin as she broke into a huge grin.

'He did *what*?' Marion gasped.

'How can you not have seen?' Azeem asked. 'It's

hilarious! Gisborne had to have an operation in Locksley General Hospital. Someone in the emergency room made a video when he arrived and it's trending *everywhere*.'

'There was no nurse on duty, so Dr Gladys made me sit with Robin all night, in case he started vomiting,' Marion said. 'My phone was almost dead and the Wi-Fi's *horrible* down in the clinic.'

The slender boy grabbed a cracked-screen iPad off the carpet, then opened a local news website and passed it over so Marion could see.

'You said cops tried to frame you for stealing . . .' Marion told Robin accusingly, as they saw a headline on the *Locksley & Sherwood Gazette* website.

GISBORNE SHOT
Hospital spokesperson says injury serious but not life-threatening.

Below the headline was a picture of Gisborne looking respectable in a grey suit and tie, alongside school photos of Robin and Little John with WANTED stamped across them in red.

Marion read aloud, '*Locksley Police Department has launched a manhunt after esteemed local businessman and charity donor Guy Gisborne was shot in the groin area with an arrow. Two ruthless youths attempted to rob Gisborne, 42, as he made breakfast waffles for his children at his East Locksley home. Brothers John Hood, 16, and Robin Hood,*

12, *then bound Gisborne with rope before escaping with cash and valuables in his $130,000 Mercedes automobile . . .'*

'Esteemed businessman!' Marion snorted.

'Gisborne's an absolute scumbag,' Robin blurted. 'That story is rubbish. We weren't anywhere near his house.'

'The *Locksley Gazette* was once a decent newspaper,' Azeem explained. 'But Gisborne's thugs threw the editor's desk out of a fifth-storey window, then told her she'd be next if she published more stories criticising their boss.'

The woman who'd given Robin the *m'smen* smiled at him and began eagerly telling Azeem a story in Arabic.

'Tala says she used to run the best bakery in Locksley,' Azeem translated. 'Gisborne demanded protection money every week. When she hit a tough patch and couldn't pay, his thugs broke in and cut open a water pipe. Her basement flooded. Her ovens and equipment were ruined, and they ordered her to leave town. Now Tala's broke, but she says Robin Hood gets free *m'smen* for life, because someone finally stood up to Gisborne and gave him what he deserved.'

'That's kind,' Robin said, nodding as he licked honey off his thumb.

'It takes guts to shoot Gisborne and rob his car,' Marion told Robin admiringly. 'But I wouldn't walk in your shoes if you paid me ten million bucks. He'll move heaven and earth to hunt you down.'

Robin knew Gisborne would be after him, but Marion voicing the danger gave him chills.

Azeem gave Marion a filthy look.

'Don't freak the poor boy out,' she scolded. 'Robin is safe here. The truce has stood for more than a decade: Forest People stay out of Gisborne's crooked dealings in Locksley and his thugs don't enter the forest.'

'I know,' Marion said, holding up her filthy hands defensively. 'But even normal guys get angry when you shoot them in the plums. And Gisborne whips people for kicks . . .'

Azeem put a hand on Robin's shoulder and gave him a reassuring look. 'Once I've showered, I'll seek out Will and we'll find the best way to keep you safe.'

Robin hardly heard this because he'd had a brainwave and wanted to confirm something he'd read on the tablet. He moved too quickly and got a blast of pain through his skull, then he scrolled to the top of the tablet screen and confirmed that the *Gazette* article had been published less than two hours earlier.

'It says "wanted" under *both* pictures,' Robin said as he zoomed in on Little John's face. 'Which means my brother is still out there.'

23. SEVEN BRIDES FOR SEVEN BROTHERS

Treetop Buzz was another Sherwood Forest attraction that went bust when bandits frightened off the tourists.

Fraying rope bridges and zip lines had been engulfed by moss, vines and bird poop. At ground level, the tin-roofed sheds where people changed into safety gear and bought overpriced souvenir photos had become a base camp for Sherwood Women's Union, or SWU.

Their food was veggie and there were Pride flags and feminist slogans draped about the big room they used as a lounge, but the number of weapons and stacks of boxed smartphones and polythene-wrapped cashmere sweaters gave Little John the feeling that politics took second place to stealing.

The women had tied his wrists, gagged his mouth and kept a brutal pace as they'd marched him deep into the forest. When they arrived at Treetop Buzz the gag came off, on condition he kept silent. They stripped Little John down to his tartan boxers, shoved him in a back room and used orange parachute cord to tie his wrists around a padded steel beam.

It was a room designed for kids' parties, with low tables, a soft-play area and a Whack-a-Mole machine. Little John's bindings had enough slack to raise a spoon to his mouth or unzip his fly, and he could stand, or slide down the post and sit. But neither position was comfortable and the tall woman – who the others called T – snorted and told him to *suck it up* when she came to empty his pee bucket.

The door of Little John's room was propped open, so his captors could keep an eye on him. While he fretted about what would happen next, imagined his dad in a prison cell and wondered if Robin was alive, the women spent the evening on recliner chairs in the next room, popping endless cans of beer and singing along to the ancient musical *Seven Brides for Seven Brothers*, with a fancy soundbar and a giant projector screen.

John spent the night on a filthy tiled floor with his arms twisted awkwardly. He was anxious and only managed naps, the last one ending sharply when a soccer ball crashed against the outside of the wall behind his head.

Morning sun cooked the shack's metal roof and left Little John with a sense of breathless panic. Contrasting with the freedom of the kids' kickabout outside.

A seventeen-year-old called Agnes arrived in a Nottingham Penguins ice-hockey shirt. She gave Little John a pitying smile when she brought in a plastic bowl containing muesli soaked in milk that tasted slightly off. She seemed more cheerful than T, so he risked repeating his complaint and she flung over a couple of vinyl-covered cushions from the soft-play area.

The beam John was tied to was padded to protect kids, but the foam stopped just above his eyeline. Up near the ceiling the metal had rusted from a small leak in the roof.

After making sure there was nobody in the lounge, John used his full height and tiptoes, stretched the cord tight between his wrists and scraped it back and forth over rough, corroded metal.

The result was satisfying. Just ten seconds' rubbing frayed part of the cord, and he guessed a few uninterrupted minutes would be enough to cut through. But there were people checking in all the time and they'd tie him in a less mobile position if they caught him.

If Little John was going to try to escape, he needed quiet time to grind through the cord, and a plan for when he broke free.

24. PEPPERS, EGGS AND PURPLE SPLOTCHES

Robin felt like stretching his legs and breathing fresh air when he left the clinic, but after a ten-minute rooftop stroll and a spell sitting cross-legged with Marion, scoffing Sam Scarlock's mushroom-and-pepper omelette, he suddenly felt weak. He wobbled as he stood, and his vision flooded with purple splotches.

'I need to lie down,' he said, grasping the back of his head as Marion steadied him. 'Sorry.'

'Nothing to be sorry for,' Marion said softly. 'Shall I get someone to carry you down?'

Robin was too proud for that, but he had to hold both banisters as he went down the narrow roof steps. Marion put an arm around his back as they turned left onto the mall's main arcade, with dead shops either side and tiny wrens making short, swooping flights under the roof.

'Home, sweet home,' Marion said, as she took off Robin's pack, so she could squeeze between metal gates, pulled over a store entrance.

The high-ceilinged space inside stretched back forty metres and had once been the discount outlet for a major sports brand.

Two of Marion's three little brothers were mucking around on a pair of escalators.

'Matt's nine. The oldest and most annoying,' Marion explained. 'The one chasing with the crazy red hair is Otto and I expect my mum is taking the little guy, Finn, to nursery.'

Most of the store's shelving and display tables had been taken out, but there were empty shoe racks along the back wall, and the sides had giant black-and-white panels, with pictures of sports stars hurdling and dunking, and cheesy phrases like, *Failing over and over is the reason you'll succeed* and *The harder the battle, the sweeter the victory.*

As Robin stumbled after Marion, towards an area screened off by a large blue construction tarp, Matt dived onto the shiny metal strip between the two static escalators and slid down head first. Robin was alarmed by his speed, and relieved when the lad crashed into a mound of swimming floats and yoga mats at the bottom.

'Hey, dummies,' Marion shouted, as Otto followed his brother down and landed on top of him. 'Your mums will *murder* you if they catch you doing that.'

Matt put hands on his hips and shouted back across the echoey space, 'Who made you boss?' before stopping at the bottom of the escalators and adding, 'Is that your boyfriend?'

'Idiots,' Marion sighed, as they neared the tented area. 'Matt literally *just* got his arm out of a sling from jumping off the roof. It'll be miraculous if he survives into his teens.'

'Most escalators have those sticky-up things to stop people sliding between,' Robin noted.

Marion tutted. 'Matt unscrewed them.'

Then she pulled back a rustling blue flap of a tarp suspended from sprinkler pipes under the ceiling. As Robin followed her through, he saw a comfy space with tons of cushions, two electric fans wafting air, and daylight streaming from a crudely cut skylight.

'The shop fronts are all glass, so this gives us privacy,' Marion explained. 'The solar panels on the roof don't generate enough power to run the mall's main heating and air conditioning, so we make dens like this.'

'It's cosy,' Robin said, as he looked to one side and saw that shop fittings and shelving panels had been adapted to make five private sleeping cubicles. 'Does it get cold in winter?'

Marion nodded. 'At Christmas I was sleeping under two duvets with a hoodie and a woolly hat. This time of year isn't bad, but in high summer you sweat buckets.

'My aunt Lucy and her boyfriend have their own den up on the mezzanine level,' Marion continued, as Robin slumped on a giant beanbag and tilted his head back. 'They're away now and my brothers are noisy, so you might do better resting up there . . .'

'My batteries are flat,' Robin said, pulling off one sneaker as Marion put down his bow and backpack. 'And those peppers made me thirsty. Can I bother you for a glass of water?'

'You didn't drink the whole time you were unconscious, so you must be dehydrated,' Marion said, as she opened a little fridge and felt the temperature of a drinking bottle. 'The electricity is wobbly when the sun drops, so I'm afraid it's not very cold.'

Robin gave no answer and when Marion glanced away from the fridge she saw that he'd crashed out with one sneaker still dangling off his big toe.

25. SPICY COURGETTE CLEAR-OUT

The good news was that Little John had an escape plan.

The bad news was, it had many flaws and he was too indecisive to go for it.

The Sherwood Women's Union seemed casual with their weapons. When John craned his neck to peer into the lounge he saw boxes of ammo, two rifles and an 80,000-volt stun stick lying amid empty beer cans and half-eaten nachos.

So, he'd wait until it was quiet, use the rust to grind through the parachute cord binding his wrists, grab a gun, then bolt for the door . . .

Sherwood Forest stretched over fourteen thousand square kilometres and John didn't know where he was. But he knew people used to bring their kids to Treetop Buzz for a weekend outing and figured nobody would build a place like this more than a couple of kilometres from Route 24.

The road to the highway would be overgrown, but he

could follow it on foot until he reached the motorway, and then . . .

This was one of the places where John's plan fell apart. Nobody would pull off the highway to pick up a random giant teenager who'd wandered out of the forest. Especially one wearing tartan boxers and holding a gun.

Plus Little John had never shot or even loaded a gun, and had no idea where they'd put his clothes and boots after he got stripped.

He couldn't see anywhere further than the lounge, so an armed guard might shoot him the instant he stepped outside. And his captors knew the terrain.

Every time Little John reached up to start scraping through his bindings, he found three more reasons not to risk it.

His torso trickled sweat as the day got hotter. Agnes checked in every so often and brought a bottle of tepid Rage Cola and some rice with spicy courgettes for lunch.

Little John couldn't see a clock, but it felt like late afternoon when the teenager paid her next visit, stretching her hockey shirt over her mouth as she grabbed his toilet bucket and saw a big brown present inside.

'Are you kidding me!' Agnes snapped furiously, trying not to retch. 'Pig!'

'I can't hold it in forever,' John said apologetically.

The sympathy Agnes showed when she'd given him cushions had worn out. When she came back, she flung the hosed-out bucket hard enough to sting his leg.

'I'm not doing this disgusting job again!' Agnes told the world, as she stormed out. 'Can we at least close the door, so his BO doesn't stink up the lounge?'

Agnes's anger drew T out of the Treetop Buzz manager's office.

T gave Little John a look of contempt as her lanky frame leaned into his room, with hands resting on top of the door frame.

'Does Gisborne want him or not?' Agnes asked, making John feel like beef hanging in a meat locker.

'My contact tells me the arrow Gisborne was shot with went deep into his groin and caused a lot of internal bleeding,' T explained, as she scowled at Little John. 'He's been helicoptered to some fancy private hospital in the capital and needs complex surgery to sew up all the damaged pipes.'

'So who's left in charge?' Agnes asked.

'I think that's our problem,' T sighed. 'Gisborne's oldest kid, Clare, is getting involved. So are his current girlfriend, his ex-wife and at least three flunkeys who seem to think they're boss. But nobody's brave enough to hand us a big chunk of Gisborne's cash without his say-so.'

'How much longer?' Agnes groaned, shaking her head.

'Gisborne should be out of surgery by now,' T said. 'But his mind will be foggy when he comes round from a general anaesthetic, and it'll take time to agree a price and organise the handover. So we're stuck with our guest until morning, at least.'

Little John realised he'd have a better chance to escape at night, but didn't let the women see he was pleased.

Agnes tutted again, irritating T.

'Sister, it's worth emptying slop buckets for fifty thousand!'

The teen snapped back, 'Easy to say when *you're* not doing the dirty work.'

As Agnes took a moody walk back to a paused *Game of Thrones* episode in the lounge, a little walkie-talkie clipped to T's belt erupted with bleeps, followed by a tinny voice.

'This is Jess at the treetop lookout,' a stressed woman announced. 'Red alert! I have eyes on Castle Guards.'

T snatched the walkie-talkie. 'Is it a routine patrol?'

'Negative,' Jess said. 'I've spotted four guards moving around to the west and I think there's more creeping up from the other side . . .'

'That's an ambush,' T told the radio. 'All sisters who can hear this, tool up and get ready for a fight!'

'I guess Gisborne's people would rather not pay us,' Agnes said, grabbing an assault rifle and fitting a fresh ammo clip. She threw this rifle to T before opening a cabinet to grab another.

'Chuck me more ammo!' T demanded.

Little John eyed the rust patch at the top of the post and heard an echoey popping sound, followed by the shack's front window shattering.

T dived for cover as a black-finned object shot into the room and made a rubbery bounce off the ceiling. The fins broke off as it landed in the seat of a recliner and bright purple smoke began spewing out of the top.

'You are surrounded by overwhelming force,' a Castle Guard announced through a bullhorn, as the smoke swirled around Little John's legs. 'You have fifteen seconds to put down your weapons and step out with hands raised.'

'Stick that where the sun doesn't shine!' T shouted back, scrambling back into the office to grab a gas mask.

'Five seconds,' the bullhorn announced.

Little John went on tiptoes and began frantically scraping his wrist bindings against the rust.

'Four . . . Three . . .'

Nobody heard two, because a sniper rifle cracked off a shot from the treetops.

'I blasted one . . .' came over T's radio.

Little John used his massive strength to snap the frayed remains of his wrist bindings, as fifty people started shooting.

26. A DELIGHTFUL FAMILY MEAL

Robin slept until mid-afternoon and felt more like himself when he woke. Marion also napped, because she'd sat up through the night watching him.

She was still snoring gently in her cubicle when Robin stirred, so Matt took Robin up to the roof and showed him how to use the showers. Privacy was a wind-buffeted tarp attached to scaffold poles and the shower head was a soup can spiked with holes. It wouldn't be fun in winter, but Robin loved it when he pushed the button and a blast of hot water soothed all his aches.

He had half of Sherwood Forest stuck to his skin and was amazed by the streams of grit coming out of his hair and gravy-coloured run-off swirling around the shower tray.

Back down in the Maid family den, Marion's biological mum, Indio, helped Robin put antiseptic cream and new dressings on his wounds, while her dreadlocked partner, Karma, cooked up a huge pot of veggie Bolognese.

Middle brother Otto got told to wake Marion for dinner. The seven-year-old's technique involved slapping her cheek with a bendy ruler, and Marion didn't look impressed as she stumbled out of her sleeping cubicle.

'My vengeance shall be merciless!' Marion roared after Otto, who squealed and took cover behind Karma.

The two adults and five kids settled around a lurid-green dining table with bench seats. It had been unbolted from the kids' area in Designer Outlets' first-floor food court, and the plastic top was printed with chessboards, a snakes-and-ladders game and the logos of giant fast-food corporations.

Robin's head didn't hurt much now, but his mind churned thoughts about his dad in custody, Little John's whereabouts and Guy Gisborne's massive whip.

The anxiety was unpleasant, and he tried to stop thinking about big issues and focus on here and now. He'd been lucky to run into decent people. He felt safe as he enjoyed mouthfuls of crusty garlic bread dunked in Karma's pasta sauce.

'This is really tasty,' Robin told her.

'You're very welcome,' Karma said, then to the other kids, 'Isn't it nice to get a compliment occasionally?'

'I prefer your jerk chicken,' Matt answered cheekily.

Marion's youngest brother, Finn, was only two and a half. Robin thought it was cute how the toddler's spaghetti kept sliding off his spoon, until he gave up and dug in with both hands.

But Marion's family was never far from chaos. Matt and Otto started bickering because Otto was picking out his mushrooms and Matt took one off the table and dropped it down the back of Otto's shirt.

Robin jumped out of his skin when Indio stood and roared, 'Can we have *one* meal where you two behave?'

Otto moaned and started pulling off his T-shirt to get the mushroom out. Karma ran around the table and yanked him.

'You sit up this end, next to me.'

'Why have *I* got to move?' Otto protested. 'Matt put stuff down my shirt. *He* should be moving.'

'Because you're a stupid ginger squirt and I'm the greatest!' Matt teased.

This made Otto tug himself free of Karma's grasp and give Matt a two-handed shove out of his seat.

'No, no, no, no, no!' Indio shouted, pounding the table so hard she made the glasses rattle and Finn look scared.

'So, this is my wonderful family,' Marion told Robin, as she buried her face in her hands. 'I assume you'll be taking up my idea of staying upstairs in my auntie's den . . .'

Robin smiled. 'Could be good.'

He found the whole scene hilarious and it helped take his mind off his worries, but he also understood Marion's frustration. You wouldn't want this drama every time you ate.

Things calmed down once Otto had been manhandled into a new spot between his two mums. Marion gave Finn a cuddle because Indio losing her temper had spooked him, and she chopped his spaghetti, so it didn't keep sliding off his spoon.

Will stuck his head through the blue tarp, said *knock knock*, then apologised for arriving during dinner.

'Grab a bowl, I made heaps,' Karma urged.

'Thank you, but Sam is cooking for my family later,' Will said, as he stepped up behind Robin and asked, 'Are Karma and Indio looking after you?'

'Sure,' Robin said, with a full mouth and still smirking because of the chaos. 'Good pasta, too.'

'The mall is guarded, and we count visitors in and out,' Will said. 'You *should* be safe, but we have a huge area to protect. So don't go wandering into obscure hallways, or exploring empty shops, OK?'

Robin nodded. 'That makes sense.'

'I made some calls to contacts in Locksley,' Will said. 'We tracked down your father. He's under police guard at Locksley General.'

Robin let Bolognese drop off his spoon. 'Hospital?' he asked, as his anxiety came back. 'Gisborne did ask the cops to rough him up . . .'

Will nodded. 'They did a good job of it. Ardagh has broken fingers, a dislocated shoulder and a complex leg fracture. The nurse I spoke to said nothing is life-threatening, but he's obviously in pain and it could be two months before he can walk again.'

Robin didn't know what to say, but he imagined his

dad scared and hurt, as Karma put her hand on his shoulder and gave a gentle squeeze.

'I also spoke to a lawyer named Tybalt Bull,' Will continued. 'He's an old friend and one of the few people brave enough to take a stand against Gisborne in a Locksley courtroom. He's interested in your dad's case and he'd like to meet you.'

Robin didn't know anything about courts and lawyers, and looked baffled.

'I don't know your family's financial situation,' Will continued. 'Tybalt says legal defence for your father would cost at least ten thousand pounds.'

Robin mouthed *ten thousand*, then lifted one leg to show a split in the sole of his sneaker. 'Do I look like my dad has ten thousand going spare?'

'Maybe we can raise money,' Indio suggested. 'People will donate to help the kid who shot Gisborne in the . . .'

'Balls!' Otto yelled loudly.

Robin hated the fact that his family never had any money and changed the subject.

'Any news of my brother?'

'Not a lot,' Will admitted. 'A pal at the police records department confirmed that nobody called John Hood has been arrested. He must be out there somewhere. I just hope we can get hold of him before Gisborne does.'

27. HOLY MOLEY, THAT'S A LOTTA BULLETS

The purple smoke burned Little John's eyes and cut visibility to less than a metre. Someone was screaming outside. Bullets zoomed in every direction around the shack, but nobody seemed to be shooting directly at it.

Not being shot was a good thing, but Little John suspected it was only because the Castle Guards had orders to deliver him to Gisborne alive.

There were weapons in the lounge, but the smoke was thickest there, while Agnes and T had donned gas masks and were shooting out of the window.

During twenty hours staring at the kids' party room, John had noticed that the metal roof over his head was only constructed for summer use, with no insulation and lots of gaps like the one that had rusted the beam.

Little John's eyes seared and his throat felt like it was being crushed. He stumbled to the far side of the room and, after clattering into a trash can, felt his way along the wall to the Whack-a-Mole machine up back.

Its melamine top flexed as he climbed onto it. From a squatting position, he put both hands flat against the metal roof and pushed with his legs. The purple smoke was thicker than ever as a stray bullet clanked into the roof, branches crashed from a shattered tree and T yelled for more ammo in the lounge.

The Whack-a-Mole creaked under Little John's weight and the force he was putting on the roof. But the machine was built for abuse and he began feeling movement in the screws securing the corrugated metal to rotting roof beams.

There was a clank of metal, three screws popped, then a blast of fresh air that was like nectar.

Little John bashed the metal several times to enlarge the gap, then bent the sheet aside. Rusted screws jutting from the aluminium scraped his bare back as he pulled himself through the hole and out onto a gently sloping roof coated with dark moss and clumps of fungus.

Little John's eyes and lungs felt better, but he didn't share Robin's head for heights and felt jittery looking down the single storey to the ground.

A burly Castle Guard came charging around the side of the shack in his bottle-green uniform. Fortunately, his focus was on taking out the shooters around the front and he didn't see Little John, squatting on the roof less than two metres above.

Little John slid down the tin roof on his bum, and held on to a rain gutter as he dropped onto a picnic patio area at the rear of the shack. Rusty metal tables had been toppled and there was sharp debris underfoot.

The shooting had dropped off momentarily, and seeing a Castle Guard so close to the hut gave John a sense the guards were winning. But as he ran across the patio to take cover in the trees, a sniper shot cracked from one of Treetop Buzz's dilapidated rope bridges.

His bulky frame could easily be mistaken for a Castle Guard through all the smoke, and the idea that an invisible sniper might be lining her next shot on him dialled Little John's fear to a new peak.

He sprinted barefoot over jagged glass and sizzled his heel on a red-hot bullet fragment, but the pain barely registered.

Little John jumped from the end of the patio and rolled into a drainage channel filled with thorny bushes and trash bags that fizzed with blowflies. One of the women who'd been singing showtunes in the lounge the previous night was unconscious on the ground less than two metres away.

There was no obvious bullet wound, but both her legs were dramatically broken. There was a rope ladder up the nearest large trunk and Little John guessed she'd fallen as she tried to escape over the rope bridges.

Her clothes and boots were far too small for him, but he tugged a small pack off the woman's back and snatched the folding knife and water canteen attached to her belt.

A ten-metre sprint took Little John to the forest canopy. He was shocked to look down and see both feet oozing blood. The rush of adrenaline quashed his pain, but he realised he couldn't get far without boots.

The forest is dense. I have water. If I can stumble a few hundred metres and play dead, they might not find me.

But then what?

Back by the shack the fighting had intensified. Three ground-shaking thuds suggested someone had unleashed a heavier weapon, and a streak of fire from a flamethrower shot into the canopy, attempting to incinerate a sniper.

From up ahead Little John heard a hollow booming sound, like the one before the smoke grenade crashed into the lounge. He sensed the motion of the object clattering through leaves, but had no time to react.

It was the size of a baseball and hit his chest with a thud powerful enough to lift him off the ground and send him crashing back through branches. His back jarred on a tree root and he was winded as the non-lethal projectile disintegrated into a grey paste that stuck to everything.

Barely able to breathe, Little John doubled up when a second projectile socked him in the gut. He tried to stand, but was immediately sent sprawling by a tactical boot in the back.

'Stay still!' a powerfully built man in a Kevlar helmet and body armour demanded.

'Give me your hands!' the woman who'd kicked him roared from behind.

She dug her knee in Little John's back and locked disposable plastic cuffs around his wrists. Little John opened stinging eyes as the male guard lifted his face out of decaying leaves and studied him closely.

'This is him, right?' the man asked.

The woman came around for a proper look. 'Hundred per cent,' she agreed.

The man grabbed a radio clipped to his body armour and sounded pleased with himself.

'This is unit eleven. I have our target secured, with ID confirmed. He has no serious injuries and can confirm he is clear of enemy base. I repeat, target safe and clear. Over.'

The voice that came back through the radio shared the triumph.

'Nice one, unit eleven! Sheriff Marjorie might give you a goodnight kiss! All other units, target is extracted. Let's show this forest scum what happens when you take on Castle Guards!'

The female guard tutted. 'We're gonna miss the fun part!'

Then she pulled a black hood out of her pocket and tugged it over Little John's head.

'John Hood in a hood,' she joked, then jumped with fright when a huge explosion ripped into the shack he'd just escaped from.

Even flat on the ground beneath a canopy of trees, John felt the heat from the fireball. His new captors shielded their eyes from a blinding flash, as metal roof sheets flew thirty metres into the air.

28. WHITE BALL, PINK BALL, YELLOW BALL

After stuffing himself with pasta and home-made chocolate trifle, Robin followed Marion up the escalator to the mezzanine floor.

'Your aunt won't mind me using her den?' he asked, as they stepped through a sliding door, into a space built from grooved shelving panels stripped out of a neighbouring store.

'Aunt Lucy's chilled,' Marion said. 'Her boyfriend works in Nottingham. She only bounces back here when they get in a fight.'

The LED lantern on the ceiling didn't work until Marion fiddled with the socket. With the light on, Robin saw a comfortable space with lots of rugs, a big mattress on the floor and a cooking area centred around a two-ring gas burner with more than a hundred varieties of chilli sauce along the wall.

'Someone likes spicy food,' he said, picking up a skull-shaped bottle labelled *Jalapeno Fire Blast – Turbo Strength*.

'Aunt Lucy brings a bottle down and smears it on everything when she eats with us,' Marion said fondly, as she opened a repurposed file cabinet and took out a lightweight blanket. 'That duvet on the bed is for winter, so this is better.'

Marion showed Robin a pair of electrical sockets by the bed. 'You'll get enough juice to charge a phone or run a laptop, but you'll fuse the system if you plug in anything powerful, like a heater or kettle.'

She flicked on a fan, because it felt stuffy, and started rolling up the thick duvet.

'I can do it,' Robin said.

Marion shrugged. 'I don't mind. There's nothing else to do. I often sneak up here and read, or watch a show on my laptop. If you think dinner was mad, you should see the terrible trio's nightly bedtime performance . . .'

As Marion spoke, Robin laid his bow on a dining table close to the light and began inspecting it. He was gutted that his most prized possession had got scuffed when he tumbled down the ravine. But he slotted an arrow, and all felt fine when he tensioned the cable.

'You any good with that?' Marion asked.

'Not bad,' Robin said, acting modest but thrilled that Marion had taken an interest in his skills. 'I might fire a few shots in the space outside, to check it's OK.'

The sport store's mezzanine was only half the size of the floor below, but Aunt Lucy's den took up less than a fifth of the space and Robin had seen a potential shooting gallery the second he walked off the escalator.

'I need targets,' he said, as he stepped out with his bow and quiver and eyed nothing but dusty shelf units and a scattering of toys that Marion's brothers wouldn't appreciate him filling with arrow holes.

'Are ping-pong balls too small?' Marion asked. 'We have a trillion . . .'

'Anything big enough to see,' Robin said, before following Marion to a musty stock room at the back of the open space. Its barren wire shelves went back more than twenty metres.

'All the good stuff like shoes and tracksuits got taken away when the stores closed,' Marion explained, as she grabbed a huge wheeled plastic container. 'But they left these behind.'

There was a rattling sound as she tilted the container. Inside were several hundred trios of ping-pong balls in clear plastic sleeves. Each sleeve had one white ball, one pink and one glow-in-the-dark yellow.

'These are ace,' Robin said, reaching into the container and grabbing a few packets.

'We found so many, my brothers got sick of squashing them,' Marion explained. 'Shall I line them up or something?'

Robin shook his head as he backed up to the escalators. 'Throw one up in the air, as high as you can get it.'

'Seriously?' Marion said.

She tore open a pack of three balls and tucked two in

her hoodie pocket. Then she served a ball and batted it high in the air with the back of her free hand.

Robin waited until the ball neared the top of its trajectory where it would be moving slowest, releasing his arrow an instant before it started back to the ground. Marion scrambled backwards, then gasped as the arrow thudded into the store's back wall, with the squashed pink ball skewered on the tip.

'What the heck!' Marion said, then shook her head and mocked Robin's tone from minutes earlier. 'Sure, yeah, I'm not baaaaad . . .'

Robin tried to be cool, but couldn't help cracking an enormous grin.

'If you put the other two in the air at the same time, I'll try and shoot both.'

Marion followed orders and Robin hit the first ball easily. But by the time he'd reloaded the second ball was low and his arrow missed by a centimetre before scraping the concrete floor all the way to the back wall.

Robin jogged after the arrow, worried the hard floor had damaged the tip. But there was no major harm and he wiped it on his trouser leg before slotting it back in his quiver.

'OK, new best buddy!' Marion said, smirking cheekily and giving Robin a friendly shoulder punch. 'Gimme the bow. You *have* to show me how to do this!'

29. CASTLE GUARDS ARE BIG MEANIES

The air was smoky. The shack was reduced to rubble and smouldering rope bridges dangled from charred trees. The Castle Guards were cocky and brutal as they looted anything of value and smashed up the remains of the Sherwood Women's Union.

Most Union fighters evaporated into the forest once it was clear they were outmatched. One pair staged a daring return, darting from cover to rescue their comrade with the broken legs. But two adults and two younger girls were caught, cuffed and hooded.

One green-uniformed guard tensed his enormous biceps, resting his boot on a young prisoner's back, while his colleague snapped trophy pictures.

'Gonna have grey hair when that pretty face gets outta jail,' the photographer taunted.

Little John's ears still rang loudly from the explosion. He only caught flickers of sunlight through his hood as they marched him blind and barefoot, along with the four Women's Union captives.

The thick mask made it hard to breathe and his pains got worse as shock turned to exhaustion. Especially the burnt left heel, where he'd stepped on a hot bullet casing.

'Get in the front,' the woman who'd kicked him in the back growled, then cryptically added, 'Unit one says special treatment for golden boy.'

A big hunting knife slashed Little John's mask and his neck snapped back as the guard ripped it off. His eyes still burned from the purple smoke, but after a couple of seconds adjusting to open sunlight, he realised they'd walked to a rest stop at the edge of Route 24.

Six lanes of traffic grumbled in each direction, with the forest canopy towering on either side.

'Move, deaf-o!' the woman taunted, giving Little John a shove. It was hard to hear with thundering traffic and ears ringing from the explosions.

Little John saw two small tourist buses with *Sherwood Castle* painted down the side and *A King Corporation Resort* in smaller letters beneath. As he got into a seat next to a driver, the two women and two kids were ordered into the back, still wearing their hoods.

A guard was last in, and he reached out to slam the sliding side door. The driver gave Little John a don't-mess-with-me stare and turned the ignition. Disco music started up on the radio as the bus crunched over gravel and merged onto Route 24.

The side windows were heavily tinted, but Little John

could see other vehicles through the windscreen. Salesmen in BMW wagons, a plumber's van with a bathtub lashed to the roof and an SUV with a curly brown dog in the back.

It was a weird reminder that normal lives were going on, while Little John rode a van to hell, with bloody feet and glimpses of a sobbing nine-year-old girl in the driver's mirror.

The Castle Guard convoy stayed in the outside lane and peeled off after a few minutes.

Exit 14C – Sherwood Castle & Resort Access by invitation ONLY!

They rode a forest track for four kilometres, then turned through elaborate wrought-iron gates and past a *Welcome to Sherwood Castle* sign.

The van got waved through a checkpoint staffed by Castle Guards and accelerated onto a wide road finished in deep-red tarmac with pristine markings.

Little John noted posts topped with security cameras every fifty metres and saw that the forest on either side was manicured, with thinned undergrowth and winding bark pathways.

They passed an enclosure filled with kangaroos and a metallic silver helicopter with King Corporation logos, winding up for take-off.

'How Sheriff Marjorie and the rest of the one per cent

live,' a woman in the back moaned, as the road arced and the castle came into view.

'Get that mask back on!' the guard demanded. 'And shut your filthy communist hole.'

30. DOWN IN THE DUNGEONS

Sherwood Castle had existed for almost a thousand years and was in a ruinous state for most of them. When Marjorie Kovacevic won her first term as Sheriff of Nottingham, the castle was a mystical ruin, with crumbling turrets and fat stone walls bedded in ivy.

Anyone who drove the muddy track from Route 24 could pull up in a parking lot with vandalised toilets and dead telephone boxes and spend an afternoon rambling over castle ruins for free.

But the young Sheriff loathed anything that didn't turn a profit. Luckily the government had recently made Sherwood and Locksley a Special Enterprise Zone.

This offered generous grants to businesses that invested in the deprived area and gave Sheriff Marjorie special powers to blast through red tape and bypass the kind of pesky planning regulations that would normally stop someone turning a historic one-thousand-year-old castle into an ultra-posh hotel resort, with lavish golf courses and a million acres of managed hunting grounds.

No accurate restoration of a tenth-century castle would have created spaces for hotel suites and lavish three-day conferences for divorce lawyers, so a trendy architect had created something she called A *bold statement that protects and enhances Sherwood Castle's original historic beauty.*

As the bus got closer, Little John decided it looked more like a glass-and-metal spaceship had crash-landed and squashed a nice old castle beneath it.

The bus turned away from an imposing lobby with a revolving door and went down a ramp into an underground car park. The first basement level was brightly lit and had the sorts of cars owned by people who stay in a resort where a champagne-and-lobster breakfast costs more than the chef who made it earns in a week.

The next level down was gloomier. A smell of rotten food crept into the van as it rolled past rows of huge wheeled bins and a gang in high-vis vests throwing mounds of cardboard boxes into a waste compactor.

'All male guests, kindly depart here,' the driver said, adopting an overly polite tone as he stopped and blasted the horn.

This drew two solidly built men out of a metal doorway. They both wore rubber boots and protective suits with full face masks. One opened the passenger door as the other showed off a ferocious-looking stun-stick with razor-sharp barbs.

'You gonna behave, big fella?' he asked, as he made sure Little John saw how nasty his weapon was.

'What you waiting for?' the other one demanded. 'Shift!'

Little John had been sitting for ten minutes, during which his left ankle had ballooned. The heat and trash smells were overpowering, and he dreaded the pain when he put weight back on his feet.

He only managed one stumbling step before crashing forward onto his knees.

'Up!' one of the men demanded, as the bus rolled off with the four hooded females.

Little John feared a zap from the stun-stick, but the two men looked at his feet and realised no amount of volts would get him walking.

His knees scraped as they dragged him through the door. After a short hallway stacked with potato sacks and boxed mangoes, one man kicked a door and flicked on lights in a white-tiled room dotted with shower heads.

As one guy sliced Little John's plastic cuffs and dragged him under a shower head, the other unscrewed the lid of a big metal tin and threw clumps of bright yellow powder at him.

'Close your eyes, numbskull!' he laughed, after throwing a generous handful in Little John's face with no warning. 'You forest scum come in here, wriggling with lice and God knows what else . . .'

The insecticide powder had the texture of baby talc,

but stung on contact with sweaty skin and seared in every wound, especially his feet.

'Rub it!' the guard ordered. 'Deep in your hair.'

Little John thought he'd pass out from the pain. Then the other guy turned on a shower, moving the head so that it blasted him with freezing water.

'Stop!' Little John yelled, shocked by the cold, but then relieved because it washed off the stinging powder.

One of the guards grabbed a stiff broom and roughly scoured Little John's back, butt crack and any other places where the insecticide powder got stuck.

After shutting off the water, the pair dragged Little John dripping wet to a windowless cell barely big enough for him to lie flat.

The light was painfully dazzling and there was a metal toilet and a gym mat, on which had been placed a sealed polythene pack containing a towel, a toothbrush kit and a disposable paper overall.

'Dry and dress,' one man ordered, as Little John shivered and dripped. 'I'll see if I can get the doctor to look at those feet.'

'What's going to happen?' Little John asked pleadingly, as the door of his cell thumped shut.

'Can't say, big fella,' one of the men laughed. 'But I'll bet you won't enjoy it.'

31. WASTING A PERFECTLY GOOD PILLOWCASE

Robin's ability to shoot ping-pong balls out of the air and slot an arrow in a quarter-second came from hundreds of hours' practice. After one-and-a-bit hours, he'd shown Marion how to take a good stance and shoot fairly accurately at tin cans and a crude target made by drawing on one of Aunt Lucy's pillowcases with a marker pen.

Little John had given up archery when he realised his little brother was more talented than him, and Robin's only close friend, Alan, preferred activities that avoided getting his sneakers dirty. So Marion was the first person who'd ever shared his interest in archery and he loved every minute.

It was half past nine and the makeshift range was almost too dark to shoot as Marion's mum walked up the escalator.

'You two have been up here for ages,' Indio said, half smiling as she eyed the pillowcase full of arrow holes hanging from the end wall. 'And your aunt's *not* gonna be impressed when she sees that.'

'Robin's *amazing* with the bow,' Marion said. 'He's a good teacher too.'

Robin felt his face redden as Marion slotted an arrow and gave her mum a demonstration by firing into the pillowcase, about five centimetres from dead centre.

'Hotshot!' Indio said, as she gave Marion a squeeze and a kiss. 'But Robin needs his rest and it'll be ten by the time you've done your teeth.'

'I had a long nap,' Marion protested.

Indio's tone stiffened as she pointed towards the escalator. 'And I'm not arguing. Teeth and toilet, now. And a shower in the morning. Your fists look like lumps of coal!'

Marion gave Robin a *what-can-you-do* shrug and turned towards the escalators. 'Later, Robin Hood.'

As Marion clunked grumpily down the metal stairs, Indio glanced at moonlight coming through the skylights and sounded concerned. 'It's kinda creepy up here all on your own. You're welcome to bunk down with us.'

'I'll live,' Robin said, as he tugged Marion's last arrows out of the wall.

'Well, you know where to find us.'

'Goodnight,' Robin said, as Indio headed down. 'Thanks for dinner and stuff.'

He found a missing arrow behind a shelf unit, then shut himself behind the sliding door of Lucy's den.

Having Marion around had kept his mind busy. His

thoughts turned back to family as he sat on the corner of the big bed and burrowed down his backpack, hunting a toothbrush.

32. BY ANY MEANS NECESSARY

While Robin gobbed minty foam into a mug, the duty guard on Sherwood Designer Outlets' watchtower eyed movement in the north parking lot. He immediately punched the emergency button on his radio and lit the intruders with a giant searchlight.

It was a group of thirty hired thugs. A dozen were on horseback, the rest on small tracked buggies, straddled by a driver with a passenger behind.

The road that once led from Route 24 to Designer Outlets had been damaged by regular floods and was badly overgrown, so nothing with tyres came this deep into the forest.

An excited crowd surged to the edge of the mall roof as the intruders formed a surly line at the rear of the parking lot. A woman trotted out on a black horse, one hand on the reins and the other held in the air to show that she was unarmed.

As the horse pulled up by Designer Outlets' sandbagged

main entrance, Will Scarlock stepped up on a dead air-conditioning tower to greet her.

'That's Gisborne's daughter,' Azeem whispered in Will's ear.

Will nodded and spoke quietly. 'Tell everyone to get their weapons. Then go see if they've got more sneaking up from another direction.'

Azeem gave a nod and rushed off, while Will held out his arms to show that he too was unarmed.

'Young lady,' he shouted down, 'to what do we owe the pleasure?'

'Don't patronise me, you rotten-toothed goat!' Clare Gisborne snapped, as she flipped up the visor of a Kevlar soldier's helmet. 'You know why I'm here.'

'There's been an understanding between your father and the Forest People for years,' Will said. 'Gisborne's gang stays out of the forest and we stay out of his business in Locksley. Perhaps he didn't explain this to you, before suffering the unfortunate injury to his *delicate* parts.'

Clare fumed as refugees and sabs on the roof roared with laughter. Will didn't want to aggravate her, but he needed to buy thinking time.

The mall was well defended and, though Clare Gisborne was sixteen and inexperienced, Will recognised several of her father's most notorious enforcers among her posse. There was no way they'd let Clare attack the outlets across an open car park, and Will felt sure he was dealing with a diversion tactic.

'We don't want to wage war in the forest,' Clare shouted up. 'But this is a very exceptional circumstance. My father has given us orders to enter the forest and extract Robin Hood by any means necessary.'

'Robin is not here,' Will lied. 'And if he was, I'd never hand a young boy over to be tortured by your father.'

The rooftop mob shook their guns in the air and cheered with approval, as Will called his eighteen-year-old son over.

'Sam, there's not enough of them to attack. But they clearly want everyone up here jeering them, so I'll bet they already have thugs inside the mall hunting Robin. Take four good people. Go to the Maid family den and *don't* let Robin out of your sight.'

'Roger that,' Sam said, giving his dad a Boy Scout salute and turning to find a dozen armed people keen to help.

'My father predicted you'd refuse,' Clare said, her voice getting shrill. 'He asked me to remind you where most of your supplies come from. If Daddy gives the order, Forest People won't be able to buy a pack of gum in Locksley.'

One floor below, Robin was about to yank his shirt over his head when he sensed footsteps moving along the outer wall of the den.

'Marion?' he asked, an instant before the door flew open.

Robin lunged for his bow, but it was five metres away and two masked women charged before he got there, crashing each other in the doorway and making the den walls wobble like a cheap film set.

'Hands on head,' one woman said quietly, pointing an assault rifle with a laser sight that left a red dot jiggling over Robin's heart.

'Robin,' Marion shouted, as she clanked up the escalator. 'Mum got a radio message from Sam Scarlock. Gisborne's people are coming after you.'

Robin wished Marion's shout had come twenty seconds earlier, but her yell did make the women glance back. Robin used the distraction, flinging his mug of toothpaste spit at them, then doing a backwards roll and lunging for his bow.

As the taller of the two women ran across the bed to grab Robin, he reached the bow and swung it to whack her behind the legs.

'Marion, stay out!' Robin screamed. 'They've got guns.'

As the woman he'd whacked stumbled forward, Robin slotted an arrow and fired at the other one. She raised her arms in defence and the bolt slipped under her body armour and made a wet thud into her armpit.

Gisborne wanted personal revenge and had given orders for Robin to be taken unharmed, but the woman on the ground forgot this as she pulled a knife from her belt and slashed at Robin's back.

Marion had backed away, but saw Robin dodge the knife, then spring to his feet.

After standing and hooking his bow over his back,

Robin used his floored opponent as a stepping stone for a parkour-style leap onto a small dining table. From there, he grabbed the top of a wooden panel and vaulted out of the den.

'Get out of here!' he yelled to Marion, as he landed hard, then ran for the escalators and dived down the middle.

Unfortunately, Marion's brothers had cleared away the mound of swimming floats at the bottom so their mums didn't find out what they'd been up to. Robin painfully banged his hip on the concrete floor as he landed, though he made a reasonable cushion for Marion two seconds later.

Upstairs, one of Robin's attackers shot a burst of automatic fire into the ceiling and roared, 'I will squash you like a bug!'

The bullets pierced the ceiling, narrowly missing some people out on the roof and leaving Marion's two youngest brothers hysterical.

Another of Gisborne's thugs came through the store's gate and lunged at Robin as Marion helped him up. But the first Robin knew about the attack was a cartoon clang as Karma bludgeoned his attacker with a frying pan, despite having a petrified two-year-old clamped to her leg.

As Robin notched an arrow, ready to shoot if either of the women from upstairs appeared, Indio thrust a pre-packed emergency bag into Marion's belly.

'They went straight for Robin, so there must be an

informant,' Indio reasoned. 'You're fast, you know the mall and we don't know who we can trust. So get Robin out of here. OK?'

'Yes, Mum,' Marion said, sounding scared.

Then she narrowed her eyes determinedly and turned to Robin. 'Ready to run?'

33. THE SWEET SMELL OF SEWAGE

Clare Gisborne's horse reared when the automatic fire ripped chunks out of the mall roof.

'You do not want my father as an enemy,' Clare warned furiously as she fought to steady her mount. 'This is your last warning!'

Will Scarlock proudly thumped his chest as close to a hundred mall residents lined up behind shaking swords, daggers and guns.

'Do I think you're gonna launch an attack on defensive positions across an open car park?' Will taunted. 'You're just a spoiled brat with a big mouth.'

'We'll cremate this mall,' Clare threatened. 'And your rabble had better stay out of Locksley until Robin Hood is in my daddy's hands.'

Inside the mall, Robin kept an arrow notched as he followed Marion's charge down the main arcade between shops. There was no sign of Gisborne's men chasing, and armed refugees stood up on the food-court gantry, ready to shoot any who showed themselves.

Marion did a three-sixty scan before cutting down a corridor with a sign pointing to disabled bathrooms. They stepped through an unmarked door, into a muggy space full of insulated pipes, at least one of which had leaked enough to puddle the floor.

'Boiler room,' Marion explained, as she ducked under thick pipes. 'We could barricade the door and hide here. But we don't know how many informants Gisborne has, or how many are hunting you.'

'Who would rat me out to Gisborne?' Robin growled furiously. 'I thought everyone hated him.'

'Refugees don't have a lot of options,' Marion said. 'Gisborne can afford to offer thousands of pounds for information. That's enough to get your kids a boat ride out of a war-torn country. Or buy fake citizenship papers, so they can leave the forest and try to get a job.'

'Everyone's desperate,' Robin sighed. 'Where do we go if we don't hole up here?'

Marion pointed at a square hatch in the floor.

'Main sewer.'

Robin smacked his own forehead and smiled wryly. 'Just when you think your life can't get worse. . .'

'I went through years back, when a big posse of Forest Rangers raided the mall and tried to arrest Mum and Aunt Lucy for releasing sixty ostriches from a farm,' Marion explained. 'The good news is, there are no snakes down here. The bad news is, that's because there are hundreds of giant rats that eat snake eggs. I guarantee you'll puke, but on the upside, the filth only gets deep if it rains, so you won't flood your shoes if you walk along the edge.'

'How long?'

'A few hundred metres. Two minutes if we're fast.'

'I'll do whatever you think best,' Robin agreed.

Marion grabbed a finger-hook at the edge of the hatch, then let it slam and stumbled back, holding her hand over her mouth and retching.

'Worse than I remembered . . .'

As the stench hit the back of the room, Marion opened the emergency rucksack that her mum had given her. She used the puddled water to soak two striped vests, tying one over her face and passing the other so Robin could do the same.

Besides it being smellier than on her previous trip, Marion found the water was deeper too. The only way to keep her boots from flooding with brown filth was to stoop, place one boot in front of another and scrape her body along the edge of the wall where the floor curved upward.

Robin had an easier time because he was shorter, but it was a fight to breathe with dry heaves trying to come the other way.

Chinks of moonlight came from drain holes as they jogged beneath Designer Outlets' parking lots.

The rats properly freaked Robin out. The size of house

cats, with slimy matted fur, black marble eyes and tails as long as his arm.

Marion was gagging and trying to avoid a last breath of sewage as she stumbled for a metal grate, where the brown sludge drained into a stream. In her quest for fresh air, she hadn't considered rusty hinges.

A tooth-grinding squeal echoed down the tunnel, loud enough to alert anyone within a hundred-metre radius.

34. ANYTHING THIS NICE MUST BE A TRAP

Little John's cuts looked less dramatic now the blood had washed away, but the burn had blistered the thick skin on his heel and throbbed relentlessly. It was hard to gauge time with no window and the dazzling ceiling light, but he guessed he'd been in the cell for at least an hour when the door clanked open.

The man who unlocked it was a different sort of Castle Guard. His bodybuilder physique was clad in a dark-green tweed suit with gold buttons up the waistcoat. The flawless fit suggested it had been tailor-made, and the guard's black shoes were polished to a mirror shine. The only indications of his job were a discreet lapel badge that said *Sherwood Castle Security*, and a slight bulge from a stun-gun holstered under his jacket.

'Mr Hood,' he said, his politeness exaggerated out of deference rather than sarcasm. 'My name is Moshe Klein, head of guest security. I'm sorry to have kept you waiting and for the rough treatment you received during your extraction.'

As Moshe held the cell door, a slender dark-skinned woman dressed in peach-coloured hospital scrubs pushed a wheelchair into the cell.

'You've certainly been in the wars,' she said, reaching down and offering a delicate hand to shake. 'I'm Dr Ivanhoe. We're going to take you upstairs and make you as comfortable as possible until the Sheriff returns.'

Little John found the doctor's tone soothing, but simultaneously wondered if it was part of a game where he was teased into a sense of security, only to end up in a dark room at the end of Guy Gisborne's whip . . .

The cell wasn't big enough for three people and a wheelchair, so Dr Ivanhoe backed out as Moshe moved Little John's 113 kilos into the wheelchair, with the ease of a parent dropping a toddler into a high chair.

Little John was rolled along a hallway and across an immaculate commercial kitchen where chefs were preparing room-service trolleys, topped with silk linens and bouquets of chrysanthemums.

They passed a bank of shabby elevators used by kitchen and cleaning staff and entered a glass lift at the end of the row, with polished brass rails and a black marble floor.

'Lower penthouse floor,' Moshe told the elevator.

The Hood family didn't go on fancy holidays and Little John had only ever been out of Locksley on a couple of school trips. So he was dazzled as the car rose out of the basement and up through Sherwood Castle's spectacular lobby, with a four-storey indoor waterfall, vast tropical fish tank and views over fancy restaurants and the flashing lights of slot machines in the adjoining casino.

After a sharp acceleration, the elevator sped towards the twelfth-floor penthouse.

'I've never seen Sheriff Marjorie's private quarters,' Dr Ivanhoe said excitably. 'I saw her once when she had a chest infection, but she came down to my surgery on the third floor.'

Moshe nodded solemnly. 'The Sheriff rarely takes guests in her penthouse.'

'You must be someone special,' Dr Ivanhoe told Little John cheerfully.

Since the mood felt positive, Little John dared a question. 'Why am I being brought up here?'

Moshe spoke matter-of-factly. 'I received intelligence that you were being held hostage. Sheriff Marjorie was concerned that you'd fall into the hands of Guy Gisborne and requested that I arrange an extraction.

'I sincerely apologise for your rough treatment. The extraction was arranged at short notice and not all units got the message that you were to be treated as a guest, not a prisoner.'

Little John sounded baffled. 'You're not working for Gisborne?'

Moshe looked offended as the elevator doors opened. While the lobby had been all bling, the hallway they stepped into was white minimalist, with pop art on the walls and a bluish tinge to the lighting.

'Castle Guards work for the Sheriff of Nottingham and Guardian of Sherwood Forest,' Moshe said pompously. 'Mr Gisborne is a local businessman who has dealings with the Sheriff, but I do not do his bidding.'

That was good news if it was true, but it posed a question.

'I've never even met Sheriff Marjorie,' John said, as Moshe used his thumbprint to unlock zebrawood double doors. 'How does she know who I am?'

'The Sheriff has flown to dinner in the capital,' Moshe explained. 'It's not my business to know why she wanted you brought to her private suites. I expect she will explain the situation when her helicopter returns in the morning.'

Dr Ivanhoe wheeled Little John through the double doors into a spacious guest suite with curved stone walls. These were designed to look like the inside of a nine-hundred-year-old castle turret, but had been fabricated at a factory in Holland and slotted into a steel frame.

There was a large bed, on which had been placed a bale of thick towels, a robe tied with a yellow bow and a basket of luxury toiletries. The bed faced a huge square window, with the treetops below stretching to the horizon.

Hundreds of little yellow birds flickered in nearby trees, gorging on plums, and a sunset made it all seem hyperreal. As if Little John might wake up and find himself back on the blood-smeared mat in the tiny cell.

He put his good foot on the room's ludicrously thick carpet and Moshe steadied him as he swivelled around and rolled backwards onto a billowing silk-filled duvet.

'All room facilities are at your disposal with Sherwood Castle's compliments,' Moshe explained politely, as he pointed to an iPad on the bedside table. 'You can use the StayNet app to operate blinds, lights and TV, and to order anything you wish from room service.'

As Moshe gave a little bow and backed out, Dr Ivanhoe slid off a bright orange medical backpack, then leaned in to inspect Little John's blistered heel.

'That's a nasty burn,' she said gently, as she took out a sealed syringe pack. 'It's going to take me a while to patch you up and a few cuts might need stitches. So I'm going to give you a shot to relax your muscles and ease the pain.'

35. MARION'S THEORY OF EDUCATION

The sewer exited into a fast-running stream. When there were floods, it reached fifteen metres deep, engulfing the car park and flooding shops at the south end of Designer Outlets. But for now, it was ten paces wide and only came up to Robin's belly.

Marion waded quickly upstream where there was no sewage, still coughing and spitting. Robin fulfilled Marion's prediction that he'd throw up. Then he rested his bow and phone on some rocks, dunking his head and swimming a couple of metres underwater, before bobbing up and flicking hair off his face.

He'd have liked time to scrub, but Marion was worried about the noise from when she'd opened the grate and set a fast pace along the riverbank in her squelching boots. It wasn't a cold night, but Robin's clothes were soaked, and he tucked his hands in his armpits to keep the shivers under control.

'We'll walk a couple of kilometres upstream,' Marion

told him. 'Nobody settles in this part of the forest, because everything gets flooded at least twice a year. It's also beautiful in the daytime, with rock pools and waterfalls.'

'You really know the forest,' Robin said admiringly. Then asked something that had been bugging him. 'So, you don't go to school?'

'I did until I was nine,' Marion said, keeping her voice low. 'But Sheriff Marjorie and her pals in central government changed the rules. Last time she ran for re-election, she got heaps of votes by saying Sherwood was full of immigrants who take everyone's jobs, fill up the schools and never pay taxes. Now you can only attend school if you have a proper address and have a parent who pays tax.'

'My dad went to a big demo in Nottingham when the government brought those rules in,' Robin said. 'And isn't there other stuff now, like Forest People can't apply for driving licences?'

'Or register to vote,' Marion added. 'We can't legally get married, open a bank account, or even go to hospital unless we are literally about to drop dead. Will wants to set up a school inside Designer Outlets, but everything costs and that guy is already killing himself, running the clinic and security, and looking after basic stuff like water and electricity.'

'Don't you get bored with no school?' Robin asked, as they reached a spot where the stream was blocked by the root mound of a huge toppled tree, forcing them to wade out into knee-deep water.

Marion shook her head and laughed like that was the dumbest question ever. 'I roam the forest with Freya trapping fish, and I do heaps of online courses. There are a few my mum makes me do – like Maths and Spanish – but I pick most of them myself.'

'Nice,' Robin said. 'With no teacher cracking the whip, I'd probably dick about playing video games all day.'

'Like my brother Matt,' Marion said, laughing. 'But I *like* learning if it's stuff that interests me.'

'Same,' Robin agreed, as he skidded on a rock, but saved himself by grabbing a shrub. 'I've got a shelf of books about archery and famous battles. And I'm kind of a computer geek.'

'My theory is that everything they make you learn at school is *deliberately* boring and pointless,' Marion explained. 'Central government is trying to numb our brains and turn everyone into obedient worker bees for the capitalist system.'*

Robin nodded. 'That would explain most of the useless rubbish they teach.'

'And teachers are total drama queens,' Marion continued.

Robin nodded in agreement. 'Like, if you don't pass

---

* This is not true. The latest scientific studies show that only 94.3% of what you learn in school is pointless, while a mere 37% is designed to crush your spirit and turn you into an obedient worker bee for evil capitalists.

this test on Tudor history, YOU WILL DIE!'

Robin thought Marion's take on the education system was brilliant and couldn't stop laughing.

'I know I'm witty and delightful,' Marion said, giving Robin a whack on the arm. 'But there are bad guys after us, so keep the volume down!'

Robin had to put the back of his hand over his mouth to stop snickering, but he'd calmed down when Marion cut away from the river bank and pushed through bushes to higher ground. They stopped on a bracken-covered spot, still close enough to hear the fast-flowing stream.

'This should do us till daybreak,' she said.

She sat down, then groaned as she rubbed the back of her weaker leg.

'You OK?' Robin asked.

Marion looked like she'd given up a dark secret. Instead of answering, she buried her head in the emergency escape bag, rummaging through packs of peanut cookies, inflatable pillows and metallic space blankets.

'I know I'm little but I'm strong,' Robin persisted. 'If you'd said your leg was hurting I would have carried your bag.'

'Drop it,' Marion said. 'It's all good.'

Robin worried that he'd pricked the mood, but Marion seemed OK as they drank some water and shared a little pack of dried apricots. Robin blew up the pillows as Marion spread a surprisingly huge space blanket over the ground, then opened one each to sleep under.

Lying in darkness made the forest feel infinite, with clicking insects and wind sweeping the leaves. They were both soggy and knackered, but couldn't switch off after so much excitement and lay awake for ages talking about random stuff.

The space blankets crackled as they snuggled closer together, and although this was the most precarious place Robin had ever slept in, he felt safe propped against Marion and thought it was cool when she half nodded off and unconsciously threw an arm around his shoulder.

36. DAISIES, CAKE, PARASITES AND PARENTS

Robin woke at first light and was awed by how beautiful the spot looked. Crisp air, tree trunks as thick as an upturned train and a soundtrack of rushing water. The foil groundsheet had scrunched up when he rolled over, leaving him with ants to flick off his cheek and squashed daisies to peel off his arm.

'Wassup, sleeping beauty?' Marion said cheerfully, as she emerged over rocks, wearing a vest and shorts that dripped from a dip in a rock pool.

They breakfasted on squashed chocolate cakes from the emergency pack, and some tiny wild raspberries that Marion had picked. Afterwards she took Robin up to higher ground, to see a spectacular spot where the stream plunged ten metres into a shallow pool.

'Stream water looks crystal, but *never* swallow it,' Marion warned, as they sat on rocks unlacing their shoes for a dip. 'The cryptosporidium only gives you belly ache, but the blood flukes are proper nasty. They lay eggs in your liver, which grow into giant worms that can survive in your gut for twenty years . . .'

'Ahh, the beauty of nature!' Robin grinned.

'Who's scared of a few billion parasites?' Marion teased, wading towards the crashing water. 'Last one in is a rotten egg!'

After splashing about and trying to dunk one another until their fingertips wrinkled they let the sun dry them off while they carried their clothes and gear up a steep path to the top of the waterfall.

It was a clear morning. As Robin got dressed, he could make out the outline of Locksley Cathedral and the rusting loops of the Velociraptor roller coaster at the town's long-defunct theme park.

'My phone's been dead in the forest, but I might get a signal up here,' Robin said. 'My brother John might have sent me a message.'

'Worth trying,' Marion agreed. 'But make it fast because you can lock on to a mobile signal to track someone. Not that we can stick around, because our drinking water is almost out.'

'Where do we get more if we can't trust the stream?' Robin asked, as he switched on his phone and was pleasantly surprised by **38% battery**.

'I don't want to go back to the mall until I'm certain it's safe,' Marion said, as she pulled her own phone out of her jeans. 'So we'll have to find some bandits.'

Robin looked confused. 'Aren't we trying to avoid those?'

Marion laughed. 'The Sherwood Forest chapter of Brigands Motorcycle Club has a reputation as the biggest, meanest gang in the forest. But I get a special pass.'

'How come?' Robin asked.

'Their leader is my dad.'

'*Seriously?*'

Marion nodded. 'My family tree is an epic tangle. Otto is Karma's kid, so not even blood-related. I've got an older half-brother who lives with my dad, and two more little brothers by the woman my dad lives with now. But it's easier just to call them all my brothers.'

Robin nodded. 'Little John's my half-brother. But same as you, we just say brother. It also explains why he's a giant and I'm a titch.'

Marion nodded. 'I know your dad's in jail, but you've not mentioned your mum.'

'Cancer,' Robin said, looking sad. 'Died two days before my seventh birthday.'

'Rough,' Marion said. 'I'm really sorry . . .'

Even after five years, Robin still hurt when his mum got mentioned. He almost welled up, but saw that his phone had locked on to a weak data signal. There was no word from Little John, but he smiled when he saw an automated message from his school.

'Now I've really got problems,' Robin told Marion. 'Apparently I'm *Non-compliant with Locksley High School absence policy and will have to report to Mr Barclay upon my return.*'

'Imagine when you fill in the form.' Marion grinned. 'Reason for absence from school: Shot Guy Gisborne in the nuts.'

The connection took time downloading junk emails and the weekly news bulletin from Robin's favourite hacking site. There was nothing from Little John, and the only actual human who'd made contact was his schoolmate Alan.

> Heyup!
> Stuff I'm hearing about you crazy crazy!
> Who knew your geeky hobby would make you
> into Locksley's Most Wanted?
> Seriously, I hope you're safe.
> Tiffany, Bethany and Stephanie asking me
> questions about you. Mr Barclay too.
> I think you might actually be cool now!!!
> Stay safe & let me know if you're
> alive . . .

Robin smiled at the message and quickly messaged back:

> Alive, so far . . . Will stay in touch.
> And tell Mr Barclay to KISS MY ARSE.

37. WAFFLING OVER WAFFLES

Dr Ivanhoe had some good stuff in her syringes. Stress and pain felt distant as Little John spent the evening watching a Nottingham Penguins ice-hockey playoff from his huge silky bed. And since room service was free he had a giant lobster sharing platter as a starter, followed by roast lamb and two slices of Swedish Princess cake.

'How are you feeling?' Dr Ivanhoe asked, when she came back after 10 p.m. with a special bandage for his burnt foot and crutches so he could hop about on the good one.

'Full,' Little John said, as he flicked marzipan crumbs off his stubbly chin.

Ivanhoe gave him another shot of pain relief and he slept like the dead.

Ten hours and sixteen minutes later, Little John opened one sticky eye and looked off the side of the bed at a large yapping dog.

Except . . .

His brain struggled to process, because the dog had a metal head and a multicolour paisley-patterned body, and there were little hydraulic whooshing noises as it bounced on its front legs, yap-yap-yapping.

Little John wondered if all the sedatives had fried his brain, as he reached out. The robot dog gently nuzzled his palm. It had no mouth, but a vibration unit in its nose buzzed, tickling his hand.

John always had trouble finding well-fitting clothes, but the tracksuit and Sherwood Castle polo shirt someone had placed at the end of his bed while he slept were spot on. And while sportswear wasn't his style, he felt a little thrill because the tracksuit had a designer logo his dad could never afford.

'You're awake,' Sheriff Marjorie said brightly. 'Good morning.'

Little John knew her gravelly no-nonsense voice from TV news, but glanced about in a state of confusion until he realised it was coming out of a loudspeaker in the dog's back. He also realised the dog must have been set to alert Marjorie when he woke up.

'Is this two-way?' he asked.

'Absolutely,' Marjorie said. 'Come and join me on the roof deck for breakfast. Take a left from your room and out through the sliding doors at the end of the hallway.'

Little John slid his feet into some pool shoes. He started down the hallway on two crutches, but before reaching the glass doors he'd realised he could walk without them if he stayed on the ball of his left foot, keeping weight off his burnt heel.

The sedatives were still having some effect, so he felt more confused than nervous when he stepped out onto a large roof deck, then jumped as a shotgun blast came from the same direction as the blinding morning sun.

'Steal my plums and see what you get, you yellow swine!' Sheriff Marjorie shouted, before taking another blast at the birds in the canopy.

A young lady in a Sherwood Castle golf caddy's uniform obediently held out another loaded gun, but Marjorie just shoved the empty gun into her chest.

'Buzz off, I need privacy,' the Sheriff told the girl, as she turned and saw Little John hobbling towards her, squinting into the sun.

'Hello,' John said weakly, as he looked across a linen-covered outdoor dining table with six chairs. There were jugs of coffee and juice and mounds of fruit and whipped cream, all covered by glass domes to keep flies off.

'The tracksuit fits,' Marjorie said happily, as she signalled for Little John to sit down. 'We guessed your size. 3XL.'

Sheriff Marjorie was a sturdy figure, almost as tall as Little John. She usually appeared on TV in dark-coloured trouser suits with her hair up in an austere bun. But in her own home at ten on a Sunday morning the hair was down and she wore furry Pikachu slippers and a Sherwood Castle guest robe.

'Tuck in,' Marjorie urged. 'I've got your favourite breakfast things. Steak and scrambled eggs. Waffles with strawberries and whipped cream . . .'

As Little John sat, he wondered why the most powerful person in the county knew what he liked for breakfast. He also got a weird sense that Marjorie was nervous, rattling her cup as she poured coffee from the insulated pot.

'You're obviously confused,' Marjorie said. 'Let me start by saying you have no reason to be fearful. The castle is my territory. Gisborne won't crack a fart without my permission once he steps outside of Locksley.'

There was a metallic ring as Little John lifted the steam-filled dome over strips of medium-rare steak. He put some on his plate, though his appetite was weak after stuffing himself the night before.

'It's usually best to tell a story from the beginning,' Marjorie said. 'Do you know that your father, Guy Gisborne and myself were childhood friends?

John chewed steak and nodded. 'You started Captain Cash together. My auntie always teases my dad about how rich we'd all be if he hadn't sold his shares to you in the early days.'

'Pauline Hood was in the year above us!' Marjorie said, nodding fondly, before going back to her story.

'The only thing Ardagh Hood, Guy Gisborne and I really had in common was that we were outcasts. The brainy lumbering girl, the quiet serious boy who liked to read and the loner who dressed in black and freaked people out with bloody teeth stolen from his father's dental surgery.

'We had our fallings-out, but drifted back together because there wasn't anyone else. From Elementary School Eight through Locksley High, right up until I moved to the capital to work for King Corporation.'

Little John nodded. 'You helped me because my dad is an old friend?'

'Not entirely,' Marjorie said, as Little John again sensed nervousness. 'When I came back to run for sheriff, I naturally wanted old friends at the core of my campaign. Guy Gisborne was easy to persuade. He knew a friendly sheriff could make his dodgy dealings easier.

'I made your dad a generous offer. King Corporation was funding my campaign for sheriff, and in return I would give them the juiciest public contracts. But your father had a trusted reputation in the community. I offered him a lucrative contract running Locksley & Sherwood Healthcare's computer systems, if he spoke at some meetings and helped get local businesses behind my campaign.'

Little John smiled as he spooned cream onto a waffle. 'My dad's too straight to agree to anything like that!'

'I mistakenly assumed that by age twenty-six, your father would have become more realistic about the way the world works,' Marjorie explained. 'But Ardagh was *furious* with me. He ranted that I was nothing but a pawn. He said he'd rather starve in a gutter than feast on King Corporation's scraps.'

'We never starved,' Little John said drily, as he folded the waffle and stuffed it in his mouth. 'But I've eaten more Great Value tinned macaroni than I'd care to remember.'

Marjorie sighed. 'Ardagh worked harder than anyone to start Captain Cash. There was some bitterness that he sold his share to me before things took off, but on a personal level your father and I stayed friends.

'To help Ardagh calm down, I asked the waiter for a second bottle of wine. We teased one another about the paths our lives had taken and dug up stories about old times. We woke in the same bed with *dreadful* hangovers . . .'

Little John made an *eww* face as a half-chewed strawberry dropped off his tongue.

'And nine months later, you popped out,' Marjorie finished.

38. I BET YOU WEREN'T EXPECTING THAT

Marion led Robin on a five-kilometre trek. The first part was tough forest, but they jogged once they began following abandoned railway tracks. They took cover twice, once to hide from a rowdy group of refugees who'd been out cutting firewood, and once when a surveillance drone buzzed overhead.

Robin felt wary when Marion said they were less than ten minutes from the Brigands' camp. If you believed the *Locksley Gazette*, the Sherwood Forest chapter of the Brigands Motorcycle Club were vicious thugs who sold drugs to school kids, set fire to little old ladies and terrorised shopkeepers.

He knew the *Gazette* was biased, but it didn't help when he started noticing orange Ranger jackets and pieces of Castle Guard uniform strung up in the trees. One even hung upside down with a body inside.

'It's a shop dummy,' Marion grinned, when she saw Robin's face. 'Chill out. Nobody's gonna harm you if you're with me.'

They walked another hundred metres before Marion pulled out a battered yellow radio. She spoke to Robin as she dialled in a transmission frequency.

'If you ever come here alone, *never* get any closer than those two big trees with the bike wheels hanging off,' Marion explained. 'The camp perimeter is protected with motion-sensing flame throwers and bear traps that'll snap your leg off. And unlike Designer Outlets, the guards here shoot first and ask questions later.'

'Tremendous,' Robin said, shaking his head.

'Main gate, this is Cut-Throat Baby,' Marion told the radio. Then, after she got no response, 'Main gate, do you hear me?'

She tutted and looked at Robin. 'I bet my dad has changed the frequency without telling me. I'll try the old one . . .'

Marion turned the frequency knob and got a cheerful response straight away.

'Sister, sister!' a youngish male voice came back. 'Stay where you are, I'll guide you in.'

Ninety seconds later a guy appeared between the big trees, giving a thumbs-up sign. He was about sixteen, ridiculously handsome, with curly blond hair. Muscles swelled under his shirt and he wore an ammo belt bristling with grenades and clips for the compact machine gun slung over his back.

Marion dashed out from cover and gave him a hug.

'I can't believe they trusted *you* on security detail,' Marion said, before looking back at Robin. 'This is my big brother, Flash.'

'Dad said you two might turn up,' Flash said as he gave Robin a crunching handshake.

'His real name is Kevin,' Marion told Robin. 'But someone dared him to drink Flash floor cleaner when he was eight and he had to have his stomach pumped . . .'

'You need to follow me *really* carefully,' Flash warned Robin. 'One of our guys put extra bear traps down. He was supposed to mark where he put them, but he was drunk, and he held the map upside down.'

'For goodness sake,' Marion said, shaking her head and looking at Robin. 'This place is a shambles.'

'Not like Designer Outlets,' Flash said derisively, as he started walking. 'Will prancing around with his clipboard, making shower rotas and giving home-grown courgettes to refugees.'

Robin caught a sweet burning smell as they passed a small clearing with two noisy diesel generators. Tangled plugs and cables lay next to a puddle like an electrocution waiting to happen. They followed the cables past battered old caravans and camper vans, most of which had been jacked up on stilts to prevent flooding.

The filthiest kid Robin had ever seen whizzed by on a mini-bike as they broke into a large oval clearing. Three wild pigs were being barbecued in a firepit at the centre, but to get there they had to cross a stretch of churned mud which formed part of a track the Brigands used to race dirt bikes.

Robin's sneaker got sucked off in the mud and Flash plucked him out.

'You need proper boots in this forest,' Flash said, as Marion dug the sneaker out of the mud and Robin felt humiliated by his unimpressive arrival: carried like a toddler and plonked on dry ground with one shoe missing.

People had stepped down from their campers to see who'd arrived, including a monstrous bare-chested bloke with a wiry black beard and an enormous tattoo of the devil riding a Harley-Davidson across his back.

'My baby girl,' he bellowed, as he scooped Marion off the ground with one giant arm and kissed her on the cheek.

'This is my dad, Jake,' Marion told Robin, as he put her down. 'But everyone calls him Cut-Throat.'

Robin decided not to ask how Cut-Throat got his nickname as the huge man swung towards him.

'Find this boy some boots from the stores!' Cut-Throat shouted, before leaning forward and glaring into Robin's eyes. 'What's this I hear about you spending the night in the forest with my only daughter?'

Robin went from embarrassed red to terrified white and tried to speak words but just made a *blarrrr* sound.

'Dad, don't be a git,' Marion said, giving him a gentle kick on the ankle. 'He's a good guy.'

'I believe that's true,' Cut-Throat said, smiling as he

placed a hand on Robin's bow. 'Anyone who shoots Guy Gisborne in the plums can count Cut-Throat as a friend!'

Cut-Throat took a phone out of jeans matted with dirt and engine oil and passed it to Flash before hoisting Robin up onto his shoulders.

'I want a picture with this heroic son of a gun! Can you believe how little he is?'

Robin didn't appreciate being reminded that he was undersized, and Cut-Throat's hair stank of booze and old sweat, but he smiled for the photo, and a second one where Cut-Throat pulled Marion into the shot.

Flash got his own phone out for a selfie and soon Robin was engulfed, getting his picture snapped with glamorous biker mums, a young lad holding toddler twins, Flash's teenaged pals, an old guy with gold dentures and finally a group shot where Robin aimed his bow at the camera, while at least thirty Brigands piled in behind, shaking their fists.

When the crowd died off, Robin felt overwhelmed by all the back slaps, high fives and strong handshakes.

'They're crazy,' Marion said, amused by Robin's obvious discomfort, 'but even Castle Guards don't mess with Brigands.'

39. THE KING OF LOCKSLEY HIGH

Little John froze, his mouth gaping wide enough for pigeons to nest in the hole.

'I didn't realise I was pregnant for six months,' Marjorie explained, as John's chest squeaked like a leaky balloon. 'I was running for sheriff. I put the side effects of pregnancy down to being exhausted from campaigning, and since I'm large the physical signs were not obvious.'

'It was you!' Little John gawped, as he returned to Earth and dabbed his napkin on the strawberry juice dribbling down his chin. 'You sent me presents on my birthday. The postmark was always China, and Dad said the government would never give you a visa to visit me.'

Marion nodded as she blinked moist eyes. 'I sent your gifts and cards via the King Corporation office in Beijing.'

Little John sounded sore. 'You dumped me, so you could be Sheriff of Nottingham and live in the penthouse of a half-billion-pound castle . . .'

'I *did* want you,' Marjorie insisted. 'Giving you up

was the toughest decision I've ever had to make. But I was desperate to be Nottingham's youngest sheriff and I could hardly campaign as a mature and responsible candidate while pregnant from a one-night stand.'

'Mum . . .' Little John said, experimenting with the word as the weirdness made him feel like he was up with the birds, looking down at himself.

Sheriff Marjorie gulped, but was determined to get her whole story out.

'We made a cover story, saying I had to return to the capital to deal with a crisis at King Corp. Ardagh said he'd take care of you once you were born, and I knew he'd be a decent father.

'Your dad wouldn't take money, because he said I was corrupt. But we agreed I could build up a university fund and send you birthday and Christmas presents.'

'Were either of you *ever* going to tell me?' Little John asked.

'After my term as sheriff ended,' Marjorie explained. 'Back then, I never dreamed I'd be elected for four consecutive terms . . .'

Sheriff Marjorie was unpopular around Locksley. Little John had heard people say Gisborne had helped win her the last two elections by intimidating potential rivals and getting his thugs to stuff ballot boxes with votes.

In return, Sheriff Marjorie turned a blind eye as Gisborne took total control of Locksley. Murdering rivals, stealing millions in government grants meant to help the city's poor and making sure his cronies were appointed to every senior post, from Chief of Sanitation to City Mayor.

This is the mum I've spent my whole life dreaming of . . .

But while the big principled reasons to not like Sheriff Marjorie were all in John's head, he wasn't feeling them.

Instead, he felt thankful that Sheriff Marjorie had extracted him from the most terrifying experience of his life, and it was hard to see his mother as some evil monster when she sat three metres away with tears in her eyes and wearing crazy Pikachu slippers.

There was also practical stuff. John had gone from Locksley's Most Wanted to armour-plated. He was wearing a tracksuit that probably cost more than every other item of clothing he owned put together. And while his dad wouldn't approve, John saw himself living the fantasy where you go to the mall with a brick of hundred-pound notes and buy everything you want . . .

Sweet clothes, fancy holidays, the best phone, a gaming laptop. A BMW convertible after his driving test. Pretty girls smiling as he parked outside Locksley High, and basically getting to be king of the whole darned school . . .

'You've gone quiet,' Marjorie said warily.

John blinked and felt his own tears forming. 'A lot to process . . .' he said. 'And after the last few days my head's in a mess.'

Marjorie nodded.

'I'm not going to pretend I'm the motherly type, but

'I'll do my best,' she promised. 'Obviously you can stay here with me while your dad's in prison. I travel a lot on business, but Sherwood Castle has everything you need: food, laundry, gym, massage, tennis, swimming pool . . . I'm sure you'll want more clothes and things, so you can take one of the King Corporation helicopters to Nottingham and go shopping.'

Little John smirked and mouthed *helicopter,* before a more serious thought hit.

'What about my dad and Robin?'

'Ardagh is a grown man,' Marjorie said, as her body stiffened. 'I gave him plenty of opportunities, but he's always made it clear that he doesn't want my help.'

Little John was surprised by her abrupt change of tone, but also understood how frustratingly stubborn his dad could be.

'What about Robin?' John asked.

'You're *my* child. He's not.'

Little John narrowed his eyes and matched his mother's determination. 'Robin is not your son, but he *is* my little brother. I love him, and I don't want Gisborne getting hold of him.'

Marjorie looked up at the morning sky, as Little John worried that he'd pushed too far and upset her. But seconds later, she nodded slowly, indicating that she grasped her son's point of view.

'I'm Gisborne's ally, not his master,' Marjorie said, thoughtfully. 'Robin shot and humiliated him. He's going to be incredibly angry and if I openly protect Robin it could shatter our relationship.'

'He's twelve years old . . .'

Marjorie raised one arm in a *don't interrupt* gesture. 'Let me finish,' she said. 'If I help Robin, it has to be done so that Gisborne never knows. And of course, I can't help if we can't find him.'

40. LEARNING TO EMBRACE THE STINK

Following Robin's brush with celebrity, Marion led him to a bunch of tables at the edge of the firepit.

She grabbed two bottles of Rage Cola from an ice box and the instant Robin settled at a table a woman in a striped apron slid him an enamel dish, piled with barbecued pork, baked potato and coleslaw.

A teenager brought boxes with new boots in three different sizes for Robin to try, before Cut-Throat arrived with a filthy boy-sized denim waistcoat. It had the club's embroidered pirate logo on the back, with *Brigands MC Sherwood* written above and *Associate* below.

'We call these club colours,' Cut-Throat explained. 'Associate means you're under our protection. It's also the first step to becoming a prospect, and eventually a full-fledged Brigand.'

'Thanks,' Robin said, warily. 'I've never really thought about joining a biker gang . . .'

'It's a splendid career for a young man!' Cut-Throat laughed.

The denim vest was stiff with dirt and Robin noted a putrid-meat and blocked drain aroma as he pulled it up his arms.

Marion sat across the table with her own pork and potato and looked furious.

'Check the sourpuss face on my baby girl,' Cut-Throat laughed, then squashed the tip of Marion's nose and made a *boop* sound.

'Buzz off,' Marion hissed, batting her dad's hand. 'Those are Flash's colours from when he was a kid, and they *should* be mine.'

The smell was putting Robin off his barbecue and he was keen to get rid of the waistcoat. 'Marion should have it if she wants . . .'

'I'm not allowed to wear colours because I'm a *mere* girl,' Marion explained. 'Only men can be Brigands.'

'It's club tradition,' Cut-Throat said. 'I may be leader here, but there are Brigands chapters all over the world and we all follow the international rulebook.'

'Misogynistic old farts!' Marion complained to Robin. 'When Brigands run their bikes, women are only allowed to ride at the back, if their husband or father is a member and gives them permission. When I'm older I'm gonna crack some heads and get that rule changed.'

'Girl power!' Cut-Throat said, shaking his head to indicate that he thought his daughter was nuts. 'I wouldn't mind, but you make all this fuss and you hardly ever ride the motorbike I got for your last birthday.'

'It's the principle,' Marion said, thumping furiously on the table as Cut-Throat walked off to the firepit for some meat.

'You remind me of my dad with the principles,' Robin said. 'And I *have* to wash this waistcoat.'

'Nope,' Marion said, smiling. 'You can't wash club colours. It's a sign of disrespect.'

'Brigands don't seem big on the idea of washing anything,' Robin said.

'Stop being a wuss and embrace the grime,' Marion urged, as Robin ate his last bits of pork and flipped open one of the boot boxes. 'After a day or so, you won't notice the stink.'

The first pair of boots were tight but the next size up fitted great.

'Better than those crummy trainers,' Robin said, as he looked down at his new boots.

Marion couldn't resist scraping her muddy sole across the front to scuff them up.

'You're starting to look less like a city boy,' Marion said, as she admired Robin's denim waistcoat and boots. 'And if you're gonna be wearing colours, I reckon we should put your butt on two wheels and show you how to ride.'

41. SAFETY GEAR IS FOR WIMPS

The Brigands might have embraced filthy bodies, but the Harley-Davidsons lined up at the front of their sprawling bike shed were immaculate beasts, with custom paint jobs and non-essential items like mirrors and cargo boxes stripped off to save weight.

'Never touch a Brigand's bike without asking,' Marion warned, as Robin admired them. 'They get very upset.'

'They look like they never get used,' Robin said.

'Road bikes,' Marion explained. 'Designed to cruise but useless in the forest. They tow them out a couple of times a year, when they meet up with other Brigand chapters and do a big run to the seaside, or a pre-arranged punch-up with a rival biker gang.'

She led Robin to a less pristine world of tool cabinets and grease at the back of the shed. There were more than thirty battered dirt-bikes, from kid-sized ones up to machines with powerful engines designed for cross-country racing.

A guy in a mechanic's overall had a bike spread out in

a hundred pieces over a long bench.

'Uncle Steve, do you ever get to the end and find you've got bits left over?' Marion asked cheekily.

The guy came over and gave Marion a hug, leaving out the hands because they were black with grease.

'You hardly ever visit any more,' Steve said fondly. 'Your bike's up back. I take her out and run the engine over once in a while. But it's a shame she gets so little use.'

'I get busy,' Marion said, as Steve moved a couple of other bikes out of the way before wheeling out her orange Honda. 'And my pal Robin needs an easy one to learn on.'

Steve looked Robin up and down before grabbing a battered bike with a titchy engine.

Marion saw Robin's look of disappointment and laughed. 'It's not cool, but it's plenty fast for your first lesson.'

She grabbed a battered open-face helmet for Robin, but didn't bother with one herself.

As Robin made his first wobbly run and turn on the muddy oval that ran around the clearing, Marion got surrounded by four lads aged between ten and thirteen. They all looked like tough guys, with *associate* colours on their backs, mud-crusted jeans and an authentically feisty Brigand aroma.

They regarded themselves as expert riders and while they acted friendly, they kept offering advice and trying to take over teaching Robin until Marion got irritated and yelled at them.

Robin had natural balance and coordination and quickly

got a feel for the bike, but came a cropper when he got cocky and picked up speed.

'Brake gently on mud,' Marion shouted, as she rode behind.

But a bump panicked Robin and he braked hard. The front wheel dug into the soft ground and launched him over the handlebars, before the bike flipped and the rear wheel landed on his back.

Marion looked worried as she sprinted over and lifted the bike away, but the four boys were all cheering and laughing.

'Nice one, dummy!' the littlest kid shouted.

'I'm fine,' Robin lied, close to tears, but gritting his teeth and trying to ignore the pain because he didn't want to show any weakness.

After faster runs around the clearing, Marion led Robin on a longer trail that the Brigands had hacked through a couple of kilometres of forest. The course zigzagged over a stream bed and she took delight in hitting the accelerator in the deepest part, which made her back wheel spin up and spray Robin with gooey river mud.

'That face!' Marion howled when they got back to the clearing. 'You look like a walking mud pie!'

The concentration required to learn a new skill had tired Robin out, and Marion was ready to quit for the day, but Nico, the oldest of the four biker lads, offered Robin a *real* ride on the back of his race-tuned bike.

'You'll fill your pants,' one of the younger boys warned.

'You've had enough excitement,' Marion agreed, as she started wheeling her bike towards the shed. 'Let's grab a cold drink.'

But shooting Guy Gisborne had made Robin one of the cool kids for the first time in his life and he wanted to show off.

'Robin Hood knows no fear!' he joked, as he straddled the back of Nico's growling Kawasaki.

'Arms locked around my waist,' Nico warned. 'Don't squirm.'

Five seconds into the ride, Robin knew fear in a *big* way.

He'd expected a faster version of the trip he'd taken with Marion, but it was totally different. Besides being noisier and more than twice as fast, Nico didn't so much ride as expertly throw the bike around under his body.

The back wheel slid out, the ground zoomed past millimetres from Nico's kneecap and at least five times Robin thought, *No way we're not smacking into this,* before Nico flicked past the obstacle with a burst of throttle and mud spraying off the back wheel.

Marion thought Robin was going to puke when he stumbled off Nico's bike. But a sense of exhilaration and the fact he'd survived made him gasp, then erupt in laughter.

'You're insane!' Robin told Nico, as he gave him a high five. 'And I don't care what I have to do to get the money. I am *so* getting myself a bike.'

42. DEEP-FRIED EVERYTHING

Robin decided that if germs and filth didn't wipe out the Brigands, then heart attacks from excessive meat consumption would.

His dinner was a vast T-bone steak, served with a heavy mac and cheese made with vintage cheddar and double cream. Then a smiley old Brigand hung a big pot of cooking oil over the firepit and started deep-frying Mars and Snickers bars for all the kids.

'It's the best *and* worst meal I've ever eaten,' Robin told Marion as he blew on a parcel of batter filled with dangerously hot melted chocolate.

Marion laughed. 'It's fun visiting Dad, but the kids here run wild. When I get back to Designer Outlets I actually *want* to eat salad and do what I'm told for a week.'

While the mall had tons of space, the Brigands' stilt-mounted camper vans were packed out. Cut-Throat shared his ten-metre trailer with his girlfriend Liz, his oldest son Flash, his two younger sons and his girlfriend's teenage daughter from a previous relationship.

Since the weather was mild and dry, Marion dragged two rusting sunloungers from a junk pile around the back and used them to make beds under a covered platform in front of the camper. They shared the space with barrels of drinking water, pallets of tinned food and Cut-Throat's elderly pit bull.

It wasn't bedtime, but Marion and Robin were both frazzled and content to lie back, letting the rich food settle as they messed with their phones and watched the rowdy evening scene in the clearing.

A guy playing guitar by the firepit had a small audience, a Nottingham Kebabs soccer game ran on a projector screen and some people who were almost too drunk to stand had decided it would be a terrific idea to have an axe-throwing competition.

'It won't end well,' Marion predicted, as one of her little brothers dozed in her lap.

She looked sideways to nose at what Robin was doing with his phone and laughed when she saw pictures of dirt bikes.

'Even cheap ones are over eight hundred quid,' Robin sighed.

Marion shrugged. 'Brigands have cleared a couple of tracks to get in and out, but apart from that, bikes are useless in the forest. And you're wasting money buying a new bike. Heaps of rich kids get them as presents and barely use them. I think Dad got mine from Captain

Cash, like six-fifty for a mint-condition ride that would have been two thousand new.'

'I *hate* Captain Cash,' Robin grunted.

But he was googling the Captain Cash website and starting a search for used dirt bikes when Marion's phone buzzed with a web call from her mum.

'She'll be lucky, with the Wi-Fi out here,' Marion told Robin, before answering. 'Hey, Ma . . . You're a bit tinny, speak slow . . . I'm doing good. Robin's fine, if a little muddy . . .'

Robin listened curiously as Marion kept her voice low, so she didn't wake her brother.

'Oh, you know, the regular Brigands stuff . . . I've eaten four kilos of saturated fat, and drunk lunatics are throwing axes at blocks of wood . . . Sorry, your voice broke up again . . . What . . . ? Of course, I can take him. Then we can go back to the mall? . . . Thank God. One night with Dad is my limit . . . I'll pass you over.'

Robin looked confused as Marion held her phone in front of his face.

'Me?' he said.

Marion nodded.

'Mrs Maid?' Robin said, which made her laugh.

'For God's sake, call me Indio.'

'Sorry . . .'

'Listen, buddy,' Indio began. 'I had a natter with the lawyer, Tybalt Bull, earlier. He's *very* interested in taking on your father's case. The police are being obstructive and saying your dad is too sick to see a lawyer. But Tybalt would like to meet with you at eleven tomorrow, so you can tell him exactly what happened. How does that sound?'

Robin nodded. 'Anything that'll help my dad get out of prison.'

'Tybalt says Gisborne has spies watching his office in central Locksley. So he'll meet you at a spot near the river.'

'OK,' Robin agreed. 'But didn't Will say this guy charges ten thousand pounds?'

'Good legal work never comes cheap,' Indio admitted. 'But your father may be entitled to government legal assistance. And we *may* be able to scrape up some money. Do you have anyone who might chip in? A grandparent, an aunt or uncle? Maybe a close friend of your father's?'

'My aunt Pauline, I guess,' Robin said. 'She might help, but no way she has ten thousand.'

'Try not to worry about money,' Indio said brightly. 'Meet Tybalt tomorrow and we'll take things from there.'

'Right,' Robin said, then thoughtfully added, 'I *really* appreciate you and Will helping out.'

'It's what decent people do,' Indio said. 'Now put Marion back on. I want to make sure she knows where she's taking you.'

As Robin handed the phone back to Marion, he looked at the animated Captain Cash logo on his own screen.

Seeing the logo at the same time as thinking about ways to pay his dad's lawyer triggered the memory of his visit to collect the mound of junk computers. In particular, the manager's revelation that Ardagh had written a white-hat security report on the Locksley branch that had never been acted upon.

As Marion listened to a set of directions to the spot where they'd meet Tybalt in the morning, Robin opened the email app on his phone, logged out of his own account and felt pleased that he'd used one of his early experiments with keylogger software to capture his dad's passwords.

Once Robin was logged into Ardagh's business email, he did a search for messages containing the phrase *Captain Cash*, and was rewarded with eight results, including one titled *Report Summary – Attached*.

It was only fifteen pages, but the file took a minute to download on the Brigands' sluggish Wi-Fi.

'Wotcha looking at?' Marion asked, as she peered over.

Robin ignored her as the file popped open on a report summary page, and he read the introduction:

> This report sets out seven critical security flaws that make the Locksley High Street branch of Captain Cash highly vulnerable to online fraud and real-world theft. Section B lists twenty-three additional issues that require less urgent attention . . .

'*Critical security flaws*,' Marion read. 'How'd you get hold of that?'

'Working at Locksley Learning Centre didn't pay

much, so Dad also freelanced as a security consultant,' Robin explained. 'He wrote this report last year, but King Corporation were too cheap to act on any of his recommendations.'

Marion's eyes opened wide. 'So there's a way to rob Captain Cash?'

Robin half smiled. 'There *might* be, if I ever get a chance to read this report without you butting in . . .'

43. LIPSTICK SMILEY BUTT

Robin cracked a big yawn as he sat at one of the tables by the firepit, struggling to eat a giant breakfast bap filled with fried egg, thick-cut bacon and brown sauce.

He'd sat up until eleven, studying his dad's Captain Cash security report, visiting his favourite hacker websites and gathering enough info to put together the outline of a robbery plan.

It was almost nine, but the camp was dead apart from little kids, a man cooking breakfasts to order and a couple of bored women who'd come off overnight security detail.

There were empty cans and bottles everywhere. One guy snored noisily in the spot where he'd passed out, and someone had pulled his jeans down and drawn a lipstick smiley face on his hairy butt cheek.

A metal door crashed as Marion emerged from the toilet block.

'Wow, I feel better for that!' she announced cheerfully, as she glanced about. 'Did Flash get his ass out of bed yet?'

Robin nodded. 'He said good morning and vanished into the bike shed.'

Marion poured coffee from a flask and put a ton of cream and sugar in. After a couple of mouthfuls, Flash rolled out of the shed on a whirring lime-green dirt bike.

'Eco-Cross Warrior!' Marion laughed, reading the logo on the bike frame as Flash pulled up in near silence. 'It suits you.'

Flash looked like he'd had too good a time the night before, with gluey eyes and squashed curls.

'Bikes *should* sound like thunder and have flames painted on them,' Flash explained to Robin. 'But electric bikes are almost silent, so they're nifty for moving around the forest without tipping off every outlaw, Ranger and Castle Guard within half a kilometre.'

Flash used a spider strap to secure Robin's bow and Marion's backpack over the rear wheel. Since Marion had longer arms, she got to wrap herself around Flash's waist and Robin became the meat in the sandwich, squashed between the two siblings with his head turned sideways to breathe.

Luckily there was only ten minutes riding a bumpy forest trail before they broke out onto a dirt road.

With two passengers and luggage, Flash drove sensibly, and the only other traffic was a motor-rickshaw straining to pull a trailer piled with illegally cut timber.

The final stretch towards Locksley was steeply uphill. Flash stopped at the edge of a small lookout area with spots for six cars. It had been built for its spectacular vista over the forest, but the picnic tables had rotted, the coin-operated binoculars were smashed and thieves had forced open the cashboxes.

'Message me if you need a ride back,' Flash said.

Marion had started checking maps on her phone and shook her head. 'Thanks for the offer, but we'll head to the mall after. Will's upped security and says we'll be safe.'

Flash nodded. 'Don't stick around after your lawyer meeting. There's gonna be trouble in town tonight.'

Robin looked up curiously. 'What kind of trouble?'

'What do you think?' Flash said, as if Robin was dumb. 'Gisborne sent an army into Designer Outlets and broke the no-interference pact. And Castle Guards blew Sherwood Women's Union off the map. They can't pull stunts like that and expect Forest People to suck it up.'

'We don't want to start a war we can't win,' Marion said warily.

'What's Sherwood Women's Union?' Robin asked.

'Best outlaws ever!' Marion said fondly. 'Imagine all-girl Brigands, with better hygiene and strong feminist principles.'

Flash laughed. 'Pinning up stripy flags and saying you stand for something doesn't automatically make you a good person. I dated this hot Union chick for a while, and believe me those ladies were *ruthless*.'

44. ROBIN TELLS A BIG LIE

They had over an hour before meeting Tybalt, leaving time to check out Robin's house and grab extra clothes.

Most of the walk was too far from the university to attract student squatters and long past the stage where there was anything inside left to steal. Locksley P.D. occasionally patrolled these dead zones, but you could hear their cars long before they saw you, and overgrown gardens gave a million places to hide.

'Forest People could make these into proper neighbourhoods if they let us,' Marion complained, as they walked.

'My dad says Gisborne's gradually buying up all the plots and turning Locksley suburbs into giant landfill sites,' Robin said. 'Big cities pay handsomely if you're willing to take trash off their hands.'

'I wish you'd shot Gisborne through the heart,' Marion snarled.

Robin thought there was a chance Gisborne would have someone keeping watch on his home, so they climbed over the gates of Swan House and crossed six back yards. When they got to his neighbour's yard, Robin logged into his house Wi-Fi and checked the feed from CCTV cameras that his dad fitted to deter thieves.

'Looks clear,' he said, as he checked the security system's activity log.

Robin had his key ready, but the back door had been left open by the ambulance crew that stretchered Gisborne away. He caught the familiar smell of the kitchen as he stepped in. The breakfast bowls were still out, the contents of the recycling bin were spewed across the floor and there was a big patch of Gisborne's dried blood by the dishwasher.

'Aww,' Marion said, as her eyes were drawn to an old family photo stuck on the fridge door. 'You had baby curls!'

She almost added, *and your mum was beautiful,* but remembered how pained Robin was when she'd last mentioned her.

Robin hopped with fright when he stepped through to the hallway. A stray black cat had wandered in and Marion laughed as it yowled and shot out of the back door.

Once he'd recovered, Robin charged upstairs to his attic room. It had only been a few days, but he felt nostalgic as he walked in. He'd left his school backpack at Designer Outlets when they fled, but found the big pack he'd taken on his elementary school adventure camp and stuffed it with extra clothes, a hunting knife that had belonged to his grandfather and a couple of family photos.

He then crammed in as many arrows as would fit and grabbed a wooden bow before heading downstairs.

'Present for you,' he told Marion. 'It's battered, but it's fine to learn with.'

'Are you sure?' Marion asked, as she took hold and was surprised by the weight.

'Wood's heavier than carbon fibre,' Robin said, as he headed to his dad's ground-floor office.

'I've never lived anywhere but the mall and the forest,' Marion said airily, as she followed him. 'This is such a cool old house.'

Ardagh's office had originally been the house's formal dining room. There was an octagonal stained-glass skylight over a heavy ebony dining table and Marion admired a glass-doored cabinet with a display of plates printed with the Hood family coat of arms.

Robin was concerned less with past glories, more with the heaps of box files, computer parts and cables strewn all over the place. Fortunately the file marked *Captain Cash Project* was easily located in an alphabetised file cabinet.

He also took his dad's laptop, because his own was back at the mall, plus a charger, a pack of SIM cards, two burner phones that his dad used for security testing and a couple of cables that might come in handy.

Robin had made a list the night before. He meant

to check it before they left, but got distracted by two message notifications when he opened his phone.

'Oooh,' he said brightly after he read the first one.

'Good news?' Marion asked.

'Very,' Robin said. 'My dad's security report said that the Captain Cash ATMs are aged machines with a number of unpatched software vulnerabilities. But I know squat about how cash machines work, so I posted a message on a hacker forum I use. This guy just messaged me back with a ton of links and information.'

'I didn't know Captain Cash had an ATM,' Marion said.

'Two,' Robin said. 'One in the store, and one facing out into the parking lot. And each one stuffed with lovely money.'

Marion smiled, but also looked wary. 'You're dead serious about this, aren't you?'

Robin nodded. 'They busted my dad, saying he robbed laptops from Captain Cash, but really because he mouthed off about Gisborne at the learning centre. It's poetic that he basically wrote an instruction manual on how to rob the joint.

'Then as we're on our way here, Flash tells us there's going to be trouble in town tonight. Which means every cop will have their hands full, while we stage the robbery.'

'We?' Marion blurted. 'Tonight . . . ? Are you high on drugs, Robin Hood?

'You said you liked my idea.'

'I thought you were talking about making a plan that we'd show to Will or Azeem. And then maybe they would do the robbery if they liked the idea . . .'

'I doubt anyone at Designer Outlets has my hacking skills,' Robin explained. 'With all the info in Dad's report I could probably do the robbery on my own. But no way could I find my way to the mall in the dark without you.'

'Are you *certain* this will work?' Marion asked.

Robin nodded. 'I reckon there'd easily be enough money to get my dad a good lawyer, and if there's extra we can split it between us. Maybe we could donate some to the clinic at Designer Outlets. They patched me up good, and you said they're always desperate for supplies.'

'That's certainly true,' Marion said, but still seemed wary. 'I know you're into hacking and stuff, but have you ever pulled off anything like this before?'

Robin nodded. 'I hacked my school and changed the report grades for me and my friend Alan.'

Marion laughed. 'That's cool, but logging into your teacher's computer is hardly in the same league.'

'The principles are the same,' Robin said.

'And your school hack worked?'

Robin didn't want to lie to Marion, but he needed her help.

'I know what I'm doing,' he said, trying to sound confident. 'And my school-grades hack went off without a hitch.'

45. LOCKSLEY MUSEUM, OPEN WEEKENDS ONLY

After the Macondo South assembly line spat out its last SUV, the blast furnace and factory buildings were levelled and replaced with a riverfront nature reserve and a small transport museum. It displayed vehicles made in the city, from a rickety 1910 wagon to an armoured limousine built for a South American dictator.

Funding cuts meant the museum only opened for school visits and on weekends, and one of the volunteers who kept the place running was Tybalt Bull. He'd opened the museum's sliding hangar door with his own key and parked his small silver hatchback inside the building, so it couldn't be seen from the expressway that ran along the riverbank.

As instructed, Marion led Robin through a blue fire door that had been propped open with a trash can. The museum space had an echo, with a World War Two fighter plane hanging under the glazed roof and rows of polished vehicles stretching to the opposite end.

'Robin Hood,' Tybalt said politely.

He'd just emerged from a staff break room, with a teabag in a chipped *Mission Impossible* mug. 'And you must be Marion. I've known your mother for many years.'

His handshake was a soft-skinned contrast to the burly Brigands' and there was nothing remarkable about him. Average size, average build. His dark suit typical for a lawyer and his wiry hair clipped short and neat.

'Have a seat, young man.' Tybalt said, as he set his phone to record. 'I hope you don't mind, but it's impossible to remember every detail.'

The lawyer's knees almost went up to his chin as they settled at a low hexagonal table with green kiddy chairs. The space was designed for teaching school parties, and there was a timeline on the wall behind, showing Locksley from its foundation as an eighteenth-century logging camp to a picture of a prince at the museum's ribbon-cutting ceremony.

'Do you play soccer, Robin?' Tybalt began.

'In PE,' Robin said. 'I'm not really a fan . . .'

'I always say being a defence lawyer in Locksley is like trying to win a game of soccer when the ref supports the other team. It's not *impossible*, but it's never easy.

'The police are in Gisborne's pocket. Locksley judges are appointed by Sheriff Marjorie, based upon recommendations of an interview panel stuffed with Gisborne's friends.'

'Sounds more impossible than difficult,' Marion said.

Tybalt smiled. 'Sheriff Marjorie and Guy Gisborne have things sewn up in Nottingham and Sherwood. But they have plenty of enemies in the rest of the country and I can appeal local verdicts in a national court.'

Robin thought he understood. 'So Dad has to tough it out. Get found guilty, then appeal to the national court and they'll get him off?'

Tybalt laughed. 'Except Ardagh is facing minor theft charges that carry a three-year sentence for a first-time offender. If he pleads guilty that drops to two years. But the Locksley justice system grinds slowly, so it will take three months for a pre-trial hearing. Another six to go to trial. If we lose, it'll take at least six months to get the appeal approved, then another three months before the appeal is heard. If the verdict is overturned, the prosecution might lodge a second appeal to the High Court.'

'And my dad is in prison this whole time?' Robin asked.

Tybalt nodded. 'And every one of those cases and appeals racks up thousands of pounds in legal bills. My ten-thousand estimate may make it sound like I'm going to get rich, but every hearing involves hours and hours of interviews, research, planning, court fees. Even if I give my time for free, the legal cost of a trial and appeal to the national court would likely be over thirty thousand pounds.'

'That's rubbish,' Marion growled, kicking one of the desks. 'The whole system is rigged against poor people.'

'What about juries?' Robin asked.

Tybalt shook his head. 'They're only for major crimes like murder. What I need is solid evidence that makes the Locksley Police Department case seem so ludicrous that the judge knows it will be overturned on appeal. Judges don't want that, because a judge who loses lots of appeals will get fired by central government.'

'Gisborne's blood is all over Robin's kitchen,' Marion said. 'But the police said Gisborne was shot in his own house when Robin and Little John tried to rob him.'

'Really?' Tybalt said brightly. 'I guess Locksley P.D. has got so used to getting their own way, they don't bother cleaning up evidence!'

As Tybalt said this, Marion thought she heard something shift behind the timeline display boards.

'Did you guys hear that?' she asked.

Tybalt shook his head, but stood up and glanced around. Then there was a thumping that left no one in doubt.

'Go hide,' Tybalt said, pointing to a vintage Locksley fire truck. 'The doors aren't locked. You can burrow under the fire suits in the back.'

When Marion stood up, she noticed a set of black tactical boots moving beneath an old Locksley tram.

'Castle Guards,' she choked.

'They must have been in here before me,' Tybalt said. 'They must have a spy in my office, because I took *every* precaution.'

As Robin put his boot on a metal rung and reached

up to grab the fire engine's door a woman in dark-green uniform bobbed up inside and tapped the muzzle of a pistol against the inside of the glass.

'Don't move, dirtbags!' another Castle Guard shouted from the open top deck of the tram.

Tybalt and Marion froze as red dots from laser gunsights jiggled about on their chests. Robin wobbled and dropped down off the step by the fire engine, just as a remarkably tall woman stepped through a fire door.

'Good afternoon,' Sheriff Marjorie said.

Then Little John came through the door behind her.

46. TODAY'S SPECIAL OFFER

Robin stared at his brother, and saw something alien. Little John wore slip-on loafers, well-fitted chinos and a Hugo Boss polo shirt. He had a seventy-pound haircut from Sherwood Castle's spa and smelled like fancy macadamia-nut hair product. They'd only been apart for three days, but he seemed an entirely different person.

Little John stared at his brother and saw something alien too. Robin wore crusted army boots, grubby jeans with a ripped knee and a denim biker's waistcoat. His matted hair was speckled with clumps of dried mud and he smelled of earth and sweat. They'd only been apart for three days, but he seemed an entirely different person.

'We need to talk, Robin Hood,' Marjorie said, stiff and businesslike. Then she snapped her fingers and pointed at Tybalt and Marion. 'Get those two out of earshot.'

'Unacceptable!' Tybalt protested, as a burly guard stuck a gun in his face. 'This is a clear violation of my client's constitutional right to –'

The guard punched Tybalt in the nose and roared, 'You speak when spoken to!'

Tybalt stumbled, but stayed on his feet by grabbing an information plinth.

'If there is one thing I loathe, it's a goodie-two-shoes lawyer,' Marjorie said, shuddering with disgust, but changing to a more accommodating expression as she stepped closer to Robin.

'I found out something big,' Little John told Robin, as he stood beside Marjorie. 'Really big . . .'

Robin took a deep breath. 'She's your mum,' he said stiffly.

John looked shocked. 'You knew?'

'Suspected,' Robin said. 'Marjorie and Dad were tight. You look like her. You're both enormous, and you walking in beside her dressed like a golfer confirmed it.'

'I'm safe,' Little John said. 'You're in *massive* danger, but my mum has agreed to help you.'

Robin tutted. 'Hand me to her pal Gisborne, more likely.'

Marjorie wasn't used to people showing disrespect to her face. She flashed with anger, but kept calm.

'As far as I'm concerned, Robin Hood can sleep in the forest when there's two feet of snow on the ground,' the Sheriff admitted bluntly. 'He can drown in autumn floods, or get hung upside down next to Guy Gisborne's collection of antique whips. But I do care about John, and he won't be happy if I make no effort to help you.'

This weird and unexpected situation made Robin's brain fire random thoughts that didn't join up. He buried his hands in his pockets and couldn't decide where to look.

'You can't live on the run forever, bro,' Little John said. 'I know you're fast and smart. But you can escape a thousand times, Gisborne only needs to catch you once.'

Robin saw the logic, but it still didn't sit right. 'So I get to live with you at the castle and dress like an accountant on vacation?'

'These clothes are from the golf shop in Sherwood Castle,' John said irritably. 'I'm getting a chopper into Nottingham to buy stuff I like.'

'You ride *choppers* now, do you?' Robin laughed. 'Dad would be real proud of your new lifestyle.'

'What, Dad's a saint now?' Little John asked. 'We went to school with patched-up trousers, ate tinned chilli and wonky carrots for tea. And you complained about it as much as I did.'

'If stuff is all you care about, I'm sure your new mummy will make you happy,' Robin fumed.

'Why are you hating on me?' Little John asked. 'I stuck my neck out to help you.'

'Quiet, *both* of you,' Marjorie snapped, as she stepped between the glowering brothers.

'Now . . .' she began, through gritted teeth, 'to answer Robin's question. He can't live at the castle. Gisborne will understand me protecting my own son, but Robin shot

Gisborne and he won't stomach me protecting you too. So this is my offer:

'I'll arrange for new identity documents under a false name. I'll find somewhere out of town for you to stay over summer. When the new school year starts, you'll be enrolled in a decent boarding school. I'll pay your fees, and give you a reasonable allowance. You'll have to steer well clear of Locksley, but the two of you can meet up elsewhere and do brother stuff during school holidays.'

Robin nodded slowly while his brain did somersaults.

'If Gisborne catches you, he'll whip you, then kill you,' Little John said pleadingly. 'My mum is the only person powerful enough to protect you. This is your only chance to live a normal life.'

'What if I don't accept?' Robin asked, trying to sound reasonable.

Marjorie aimed a hand towards the door. 'I have no beef with you, Robin. You can walk away, but my offer of protection expires when I leave this room. If Gisborne catches you, that's your problem. If Rangers arrest you, that's your problem. If you get sick and need a hospital, that's your problem.'

'Don't be like Dad,' Little John begged. 'Swallow your pride and take what's on offer.'

Robin felt boiling hot, with sweat streaking down his neck and a lump in his throat.

He was afraid of Gisborne, and this was probably the only way he could ever be safe. He reckoned he could tolerate the new name and the boarding school, but the idea of accepting Marjorie's offer didn't feel right and his brain was in tangles until the reason finally snapped into focus:

Sheriff Marjorie is a terrible person.

She'll do whatever it takes to get what she wants, and she admits she doesn't care about me . . . If I accept the offer, she'll own me. Go to a school she picks. Spend holidays with people she picks. If I get in trouble, I answer to her. If I want anything, I have to ask her.

The idea of going back to the mall with Marion and seeing people like Indio and Will made Robin feel good. Being in a strange place where he didn't know a soul and Sheriff Marjorie pulled all the strings felt like a black hole.

'Thanks for thinking up a plan to help me,' Robin told Marjorie. 'But my answer is no.'

Marjorie seemed relieved, because looking after any kid is a pain and she'd saved six years of boarding-school fees. But Little John looked furious.

'See you at your funeral, dumbass,' he growled, then shook his head as he followed his mum outside.

47. ONE DASH OF EMOTIONAL BLACKMAIL

Tybalt's nose was a bloody mess and Marion called a taxi because there was no way he could drive. Robin had disappeared, and she found him in front of the museum, slumped on a bench facing swaying reed beds in the adjoining nature reserve.

'I wish my mum was still around,' Robin sniffed.

Marion didn't know what to say, but put an arm around Robin's back while keeping a wary eye out. The area wasn't busy, but Robin's face had been on the news and the front of the museum faced a wooden boardwalk where people jogged or passed through when they took toddlers to feed ducks in the reserve.

'We can't stay in the open, Robin,' Marion said gently. 'Let's head back to Designer Outlets. You'll feel less stressed once you've cleaned up. We can find some nice food on the roof and watch a movie or something.'

Robin looked up sharply, rubbing soggy eyes then shaking his head determinedly.

'I want to do stuff, not watch stuff,' he said firmly. 'I need money to help my dad.'

'You're in the wrong frame of mind,' Marion said. 'Show your plan to Will. He's done heaps of robberies.'

'Stick-ups with guns isn't hacking,' Robin said. 'That's like comparing boxing with chess.'

Marion sighed and gave him another squeeze.

'If you're backing out, I'll do the robbery on my own,' Robin said. 'Locksley has eighty thousand empty houses I can hide in overnight. Could you meet me and take me back to Designer Outlets in the morning?'

Marion smiled. 'You do tend to fall into ravines when I'm not guiding you.'

Robin looked at her with pleading eyes, and Marion softened because his expression and his dirty face were adorable . . .

'Fine, I'll help with your stupid robbery,' she groaned. 'But if I get busted and wind up in juvenile boot camp with some brute making me do push-ups in mud, you'll be *totally* off my friends list.'

48. DROP IN ON AN OLD PAL

While most of Locksley crumbled, a couple of smart new developments had cropped up on the outskirts, providing modern homes for people like the Chief of Police, the CEO of Locksley Redevelopment Corporation and a variety of clean-cut folks shipped in to make Gisborne's front companies look respectable.

One such house, with a Spanish colonial vibe and a Range Rover on the driveway, belonged to Nasha Adale, the controller of Locksley's public bus system. Her oldest child, Alan, had just finished a dreary Monday afternoon at Locksley High and he was curious about a slight gym-locker smell as he slotted his key in the front door.

'Hey,' Robin whispered.

Alan jumped back, then glanced around and saw his long-term friend and a girl with striking blue eyes squatting behind shrubs.

'Made me jump,' Alan moaned, then smiled. 'Good to know you're alive.'

'This is Marion,' Robin said. 'Are you home alone?'

Alan nodded. 'Mum picks my sister up from rugby practice and gets in about six o'clock. Dad'll be home a while after that.'

'Perfect,' Robin said, as he stepped towards the open front door.

Alan blocked his path into an immaculate white-tiled hallway. 'Not in those boots. You gotta come around the side.'

He jogged into the house, out through sliding patio doors at the back and took the bolt off a gate at the side of the house.

'My parents will figure if you trail muck everywhere,' Alan explained. 'We had Locksley P.D. here asking me questions about your habits. My ma is tight with Gisborne's people and she's lecturing me: *If you know about that hoodlum boy Robin Hood, you tell the police or there'll be big trouble!*'

'Please don't snitch.' Robin smiled, knowing his oldest friend wouldn't.

Marion hadn't seen this kind of house before and gawped as she walked past the hot exterior blast from air conditioners and into a garden with a pool and a trendy wood-fired oven.

'Use the pool shower,' Alan said, pointing to a slatted wooden cage up against the back of the house. 'I'll grab towels.'

Marion showered first. Robin gave her a spare T-shirt

from his bag of clothes, but it was short, so Alan found some shorts and a two-seasons-old Macondo United shirt that fitted her fine.

Alan and Marion sat with their feet in the pool eating chips and dip, while Robin shampooed twice to get all the mud out of his hair.

'Your dad still got that 3D printer?' Robin asked, reaching down to grab chips as he towelled off.

'In the garage, with all the other junk he never uses.'

The two boys headed to a triple garage, home to jet skis, an electric piano, hunting gear and soccer goals.

'You printing keys for another robbery?' Alan asked. 'Hope it works better than your fiasco in Mr Barclay's office . . .'

Robin almost swallowed his tongue and was thankful Marion had stayed out by the pool.

'Don't mention that,' Robin hissed. 'Marion thinks I know what I'm doing.'

'Poor deluded creature.' Alan laughed, then took the cube-shaped printer upstairs to his room, where it wouldn't immediately get spotted if a parent arrived home freakishly early.

3D printers are fiddly to set up. Robin's hacker pal had hooked him up with the digital design for a tool that engineers use to open cash machines, but the printer's error light kept flashing, until Robin realised Alan's dad hadn't run the cleaning procedure after the only time he'd used it.

After ten minutes unscrewing a nozzle and picking chunks of melted plastic out of the filament dispenser, Robin started his print job and headed downstairs, where Alan and Marion had crashed in front of a true-life car-chase show called *Triple-Digit Speed*.

'You know the graffiti wall behind the gym at school?' Alan asked.

'Sure.' Robin nodded as his eyes hunted for his half-drunk tin of Rage Cola.

'There's a massive new mural,' Alan said. 'It says *Robin Hood Lives*. And the double-o in Hood is drawn like a pair of balls with an arrow sticking out of them.'

Marion laughed so hard that her feet flew up in the air. 'Seriously?'

'Get out of town,' Robin said, as he flopped over a couch.

'You've attained legend status,' Alan said. 'I'll take a picture next time I go around there.'

'How much longer for your 3D lever thingy to print?' Marion asked.

'Half an hour if it doesn't crash,' Robin said, as a car on the TV smashed through a barrier and got obliterated by a truck going the opposite way.

'You guys can stick around till just before six,' Alan said. 'But you'll have to give me time to clear towels and stuff. Cos I'm a dead man if my parents find out you were here.'

'Yeah,' Robin said, shaking his head slowly. '*You're* the one whose life is in danger . . .'

49. THE LOVELY SHIMMERING UNICORN

It's hard sneaking around a busy part of town when your face has been all over the news. But Robin was short, and Alan's ten-year-old sister was above average height, so he slipped nicely into her striped leggings, pink Converse All Stars and a lemon hoodie with a shimmering unicorn on the front.

His scruffy hair passed for girly once Marion swept it back, fixed a couple of hair grips in it and packed the mess under a baseball cap.

'It's not *that* funny,' Robin protested, as Alan rolled around his bedroom floor clutching his sides and claiming that he was *going to die.*

'I think he's got a *great* bum for leggings,' Marion grinned.

Marion's battered forest boots looked wrong with Alan's shorts and hockey shirt. He had clown feet and his sister's shoes were too small, but Alan dug some suitably sized Nikes out of years-old junk at the bottom of his wardrobe.

Alan gave hugs and wished them luck when they left. Nobody batted an eye at two girls riding a city bus into the centre of Locksley.

After stepping off at the semi-derelict transit terminal, they took a short walk, hiding Marion's wooden bow and Robin's heavy bag of clothes on an overgrown lot behind Hipsta Donut.

Then they split up, Marion heading for Locksley's civic square six blocks west, and Robin cutting through nettles into the back lot of Hipsta's. He caught a dose of nerves and the stupid jingle as he stepped through the automatic doors of Captain Cash.

Don't take fright when money's tight . . .

'We close in eight minutes,' the security officer warned Robin as he swept into the main part of the store.

He'd assumed it would be quiet this near closing time, but the place was a zoo, busier than when he'd visited with his dad.

He walked between rows of cabinets, lowering his gaze when he passed Rhongomaiwenua, unlocking a sliding glass panel and retrieving an Xbox controller for a kid with a cast on his wrist.

'This is your last one ever,' his mum warned. 'You can't hurl the pad every time you lose . . .'

It was quieter at the rear of the store, where the two ATMs stood back to back and glass cabinets gave way to raised platforms displaying larger items like lawnmowers and kid-sized electric cars.

Robin spent a few minutes pretending to be interested in a box filled with wetsuits, while two toddlers tussled over the driver's seat of a mini police car.

'This store is now closed,' a recorded announcement began. 'Please leave the premises, or move to the front of the store to purchase your items. Captain Cash is available twenty-four hours a day online. So why not check us out . . .'

A dad came over and retrieved the two kids. After a backwards glance down the row of cabinets, Robin ducked through a rack of used skis and squatted in a shadowy gap between a ride-on mower and the box of wetsuits.

50. MA ON THE WARPATH

Locksley Civic Square was dominated by City Hall, a grand affair built in the days when property taxes gushed in from giant auto makers. Now the windows were cracked and dirty and the elaborate rooftop clock shaped like a car's front grille was stuck at half past two.

The sun was dipping as Marion hid in an alcove on marble steps leading up to Locksley Art Gallery's permanently boarded entrance. It felt tense, with more people milling around than you'd expect two hours after Central Court and City Hall closed. New graffiti had just been sprayed at the base of the statue of town founder Winston Locksley:

END POLICE CORRUPTION

Indio had sent her daughter five increasingly fraught texts and Marion took a deep breath before playing her mum's latest voicemail.

'*Marion, you are pushing your luck!*' Indio snapped. '*I don't know what you and Robin are up to, but it's a quarter past seven and Tybalt said he left you at lunchtime. I demand to know where you are. I got your text telling me not to worry, but three words is not good enough! Stop dodging my calls and ring me the instant you get this.*'

Marion shuddered as she tapped five to delete.

Indio was worried, and Marion didn't like lying. But her mum would only get madder if she called back and explained that she was hiding at the edge of Civic Square waiting for trouble to break out, at which point she'd call Robin, so he could use the fact that all the cops would be distracted to help stage a robbery . . .

Another message pinged. This one from Marion's brother, Flash.

> **Why do you want to know when the trouble is starting?**
> **Your old lady is going bonkers, calling everyone asking if they've seen you.**

Marion groaned as she texted back:

> **PLEASE tell me when it is supposed to kick off.**
> **I'll explain why tomorrow.**

Flash replied immediately.

> **Any minute now**
> **Indio's gonna ground you for a month.**

Marion texted back:

> **Cheers for answering**

I'm betting three months :-)

Marion smiled at her own joke, but felt stressed. Even if everything went to plan, she'd still be in big trouble.

She wondered if she was an idiot as she tilted her head up and saw the beginning of sunset. Robin was cool, but she was putting her head on the chopping block for someone she'd known less than a week.

When she looked back down Marion noticed heaps of people marching into the square via an archway between the office buildings. There were a few people she recognised, including the woman who sprinted towards the centre of the square and fearlessly climbed Sir Winston Locksley with a long flag draped over her back.

An ominous rumbling came from outside the square as Marion tapped her phone and found Robin's name, so she was ready to message him. There were now more than a hundred Forest People in the square, with more coming from all directions.

A half-brick got lobbed through one of City Hall's windows and a cheer went up as the flag unfurled, tied around Sir Winston's neck. The flag had a tree with branches shaped like a fist and the slogan:

FOREST SCUM BITES BACK!

Marion felt proud seeing her people standing up for themselves. She wanted to run down the gallery steps and join the mob, but she had a job to do and sent a message to Robin.

Kicking off now. Looks EPIC!

Some of the Forest People moving into the centre of the square were chanting *Robin Hood* and hurling ripe plums at an office occupied by one of Gisborne's companies, but their chants were drowned out when the ominous noise grew deafening.

Black Bess roared into the square, blasting its horn as it skimmed the bottom of the steps a few metres from Marion's alcove.

It mounted the pavement and drove in a wide arc, sending protestors scattering as it picked up speed, then went straight for the steel-and-glass facade of Locksley Central Court.

Marion gasped as the enormous bull bars of Gisborne's stolen ride smashed through plate glass into the court lobby, obliterating X-ray barriers and skidding to a halt near the foot of an escalator.

The courthouse alarms had erupted, and cop sirens were getting closer.

Marion was supposed to sprint back and help Robin, but she was engrossed as Black Bess's engine cut. Then shocked when two young men jumped out.

They wore ice-hockey masks, but Marion knew her brother from his posture and swaggering walk. She wasn't sure whether to feel proud or horrified.

'Everyone get back,' Flash yelled into the square.

His passenger ran over shattered glass and vanished into the crowd, while Flash took a mini gas blowtorch from his trouser pocket, lit the flame and tossed it into the back of the SUV. They must have sprayed fuel inside, because the whole interior flared instantly, and Flash almost got hit by a whoosh of flame venting through the side window.

'Gisborne, you suck!' he shouted, before scrambling out to back-slapping rapture from the crowd.

Gisborne's car burning in the lobby of Locksley's corrupt courthouse felt like a perfect symbol of protest and sent the crowd into a frenzy. Some smashed glass and sprayed graffiti. Others charged up the steps of City Hall, trying to force their way inside.

51. MEANWHILE, SIX BLOCKS EAST

Robin sat dead still, staring at his leggings and pink Converse as the day's final customers cashed cheques and loaded a used treadmill into a truck. A security guard walked every aisle, picking a lost cardigan off the floor and sticking her head into the customer bathroom. But she didn't stoop low enough to see the twelve-year-old hiding.

Isla the manager was the last out, switching off ceiling lights but leaving the ones inside the glass cabinets. Robin turned slightly, so he could see as she set the intruder alarm. Once outside, Isla slammed the shutter over the main entrance and drove away in the last car on the lot.

Now the alarm's motion sensors were armed, Robin had to be even more careful not to move. He stared at the burner phone he'd picked up in his dad's office, waiting for Marion's message, unsure whether he'd be there for minutes or hours.

His back ached, the leggings itched and a flashing red

light coming from the sign on top of Hipsta Donut gave his hiding place a seedy vibe. Then he got a bleep.

Kicking off now. Looks EPIC!

'All right,' Robin said, peeling the leggings away from his bum as he scrambled out of hiding.

He put on cleaning gloves to hide fingerprints, then stepped between the skis and made two strides before the alarm box by the main entrance triggered. The box buzzed gently, allowing thirty seconds to enter a code before the main bell erupted and an automated call went to Locksley P.D.

Ardagh's report listed the intruder alarm as the branch's number-one security weakness. It noted that seventy-three employees had been given codes for the alarm in the nine years since it had been installed. Some employees admitted sharing codes with others. Codes hadn't been deleted from the system when employees quit, and staff had been allowed to pick stupidly easy numbers like 1234, or 6666.

Robin tapped 1369 – the four corners of the numeric pad – followed by the *enter* key. The buzzing stopped, and the amber display panel flashed 'SYSTEM OPEN'.

He was momentarily jolted by flashing blue lights, but the cop car was rolling out of Hipsta Donut next door, not coming after him.

Robin felt pleased as he ran back to grab a little bag with his laptop and hacking gear out of the hiding spot. Four wailing cop cars shot down the High Street and customers were stepping out of Hipsta Donut, curious about the sudden chaos.

The two ATMs stood next to each other. One facing into the store and one with the control panel facing out into the car park.

Ardagh's report said the ATMs were fourteen-year-old Higgs QT-3.14s. Their armour-plated cashboxes had a maximum capacity of two hundred thousand pounds and both lived behind neon-orange Captain-Cash-branded vanity panels.

Major banks had phased out the QT-3.14 because of the very thing Robin was about to do. But thousands of the aged machines still spat out money in convenience stores, service stations and more than eighty Captain Cash branches.

The T-shaped bar Robin printed at Alan's house slotted into a hole at the base of the indoor machine. When he turned the handle, a clasp popped and the wobbly plastic panel around three sides sprang loose, exposing the machine's innards.

'So far, so good . . .' Robin told himself as he dragged the panel clear and knelt down to start work.

52. THE GEEKS SHALL PROSPER

Every cash machine has three sections. The keypad and screen module at the top and an armoured cashbox in the base. The brain linking these two parts is a regular Windows computer, which can be hacked. Especially if it's an elderly ATM running out-of-date software.

Robin rested his laptop on the carpet and ran a long lead into the network port on the rear of the ATM. He was no ace hacker, but experienced enough to download software and follow instructions.

The network and USB ports on the QT-3.14's computer were disabled, but one network socket had to stay live, connecting to the outside world to check customer account balances before delivering cash.

Hackers had found a way to overwrite the QT-3.14's software using this open port. Robin started a remote software update program he'd pre-installed on his dad's laptop, clicking *yes* when it asked if he wanted to **Install BIOS on remote terminal.**

The BIOS (Basic Input/Output System) is a tiny program that runs when you first switch a computer on, doing stuff like detecting the keyboard and switching on cooling fans. Critically for Robin's hack, the BIOS also chooses which drive the operating system boots from.

The update took fifty anxious seconds, before asking:

`Reboot terminal with new BIOS? Y/N`

Robin plugged a USB stick into a port at the back of the computer. If the hacked BIOS had installed correctly, it would reactivate the computer's USB socket and run hacked software from this USB stick, rather than the hard drive inside the machine.

Robin was comforted by a flickering light on the USB drive, as he rose onto one knee and studied the ATM screen. It had two blinking >> cursors and a *Please Wait* message. Occasionally the screen flashed, or some green text scrolled by, too fast to read.

He was utterly focused, and startled when a hand rapped on the window close by.

'Let me in,' Marion growled. 'I've been thumping on the back door.'

'Sorry,' Robin gasped.

He scooted off the carpet and crashed the bar across a fire door at the rear.

'What's it like out there?' he asked.

'They drove Black Bess into Central Court and blew it up.'

'Wow!' Robin grinned.

'Now they're fighting cops, running wild through City Hall and trashing Gisborne's private offices.'

'Should know if my hack has worked any second now,' Robin said. 'And put your gloves on before you start touching stuff.'

The ATM had finished booting and apparently the anonymous hacker who rewrote the QT-3.14 operating software had a sense of humour. The machine's usual options to *check balance* or *withdraw money* were now replaced with a green smiley face and:

FREE MONEY!
<<< Yes   No >>>

Robin returned the machine's smile as he tapped *yes*.

There was a beep, then a noise like a seatbelt coming undone as the armoured door of the cashbox popped. Hinges squealed as Robin swung it open, then he stuck his head inside and saw four slots, each with a grey plastic cartridge like the ones that go into a photocopier.

But instead of white paper, Robin eased the top one out and eyed a tray stacked with hundred-pound notes. A guide along one side showed roughly how much cash was left.

'Nineteen thousand in this tray,' Robin said, as Marion leaned in for a peek.

'Robin,' she said, laughing in triumph. 'that looks even more beautiful than you in your pearlescent unicorn hoodie.'

53. ALL ITEMS 100% OFF

The second tray was empty, but the third had £11,000 in twenties, and the fourth was a jackpot.

'Full tray, fifty thousand squids!' Robin beamed.

'How are we gonna carry all this?' Marion asked.

Robin laughed. 'I guess there are worse problems to have. Go look for a bag while I do the other machine.'

Marion nodded. 'There's four dirt bikes over there. The keys might be behind the counter somewhere.'

'Good thinking,' Robin said, as he looked outside, making sure nobody was using the other machine.

A young man and woman in muddy forest boots were running across the front lot, holding hands. They were glancing back like someone was chasing them, so there was no way they'd be stopping for cash.

Once he'd popped the second vanity panel, Robin swung it around and pushed it up against the plate glass, so nobody could see him from outside. This machine looked identical, except it had a back-up screen inside the case, so that an engineer didn't have to keep walking outside.

As Robin plugged in the laptop and repeated the hack, Marion slid over the service counter and began searching drawers and cupboards.

'There's a safe back here,' Marion said. 'It must be where they keep watches, and wedding rings.'

'I don't have any safe-cracking skills,' Robin said. 'How are yours?'

'Non-existent,' Marion admitted, then her tone changed as she opened a drawer. 'Oooh, hello!'

Back on the customer side of the counter, Marion threw a big nylon equipment bag at Robin's feet then moved towards the bikes holding a pouch full of numbered keys.

'The good news is I've found the key to the white dirt bike you liked on the website,' Marion said. 'But the tank's empty, so you're getting the blue one.'

As the back-up screen on the second ATM popped up with the *Free Money* option, the store ripped with the sound of a motorbike engine. Marion drove it cautiously off a low plinth and almost clipped a fish tank as she rode down a narrow aisle towards Robin.

'How does it look?' she asked.

'Suits you,' Robin grinned, as he proudly showed her the first cartridge from the second machine, with £31,000 in fifties. 'Can you start bagging up?'

A cop car rolled to a stop on the other side of the high street as Marion packed the money in the equipment bag.

It set them both on edge, but there was no sign of the two officers taking an interest in Captain Cash.

As Robin opened the final tray, his on-the-fly calculation was that they'd taken £120,000 from the two machines.

'I need something to tie this bag onto the bike,' Marion said, glancing around.

Once he'd bagged his laptop, leads and USB drive, Robin dived onto the counter and looked at the cashier terminals and wastepaper baskets underneath. He spotted a small black box at the far end, slid over on his belly and pulled all the cables out of the back.

'CCTV,' Robin explained, as he tossed the box into the big bag with the money. 'Under the counter, not even secured by a locking bracket . . .'

Marion smiled, but the cop car across the street was making her uncomfortable and she moved closer to the window and peeked.

'I think they're searching for someone,' she said. 'One officer got out and shone her torch around. Now they're back in the car, talking on the radio. Shall we wait here until they're gone?'

Robin shook his head. 'They won't see if we ride out the back door.'

'Two of us, two bags and your bow,' Marion said. 'We'll be laden before we grab the stuff we dumped in the back lot.'

As she eyed a reel of heavy line in Captain Cash's

section, Robin dashed out the back door and crossed to the lot behind, where they'd left their forest clothes and the stuff he'd brought from home.

By the time he'd scrambled over the bushes, grabbed the two bags and jogged back onto the Captain Cash lot, Marion had secured the money bag and pushed the bike up to the rear fire door.

'Ready to roll?' she asked as Robin got close.

With ten things on their minds and a constant backdrop of police sirens, neither of them had noticed one siren getting seriously loud. But they knew it when a big police SUV turned onto the Captain Cash lot, blazing its rooftop searchlight through the front of the store.

54. SOMETHING TO PROTEST ABOUT

Robin dived for cover, scraping his palms as he hit the tarmac.

A cop from the car parked across the street was running towards Hipsta Donut with her gun drawn, while the SUV with the searchlight stopped at the end of a short alleyway between the donut store and Captain Cash, its dazzling beam lighting up air vents and wheelie bins.

As a second cop jumped out of the searchlight car, Robin realised the officer from across the street was circling around the side of Hipsta to block the alleyway from the other end. But his position at the rear of the two buildings gave no view down the alleyway.

'I don't know who they're after, but it's not us,' Robin said, as he reached Marion in the doorway and stood up, wiping shards of grit off his gloved hands.

'But they'll see us if we ride off,' she said. 'Let's go back inside and wait.'

'You have no way out,' a cop shouted to whoever was

in the alleyway. 'Step out from between the trash cans with your hands raised.'

The cops with the searchlight had pulled onto the lot after spotting a young couple squatting in the alleyway – the same pair Robin had seen running before he started work on the second ATM.

The cops assumed the couple were now trapped in the alleyway with officers blocking both ends. But they'd managed to climb on one of the bins and pull themselves onto Captain Cash's flat roof.

Robin and Marion heard footsteps on the metal roof above as they were about to go back inside, then they froze in shock as two bodies leaped off the roof, from directly above them.

The forest couple rolled expertly as they landed on the parking lot. But they'd been spotted crossing the roof by the officer who'd stayed with the car across the street, and he radioed his colleagues as he started his engine and shot across the four-lane high street to intercept.

As Robin and Marion dived inside and slammed the fire door, the cop who'd been blocking the rear of the alleyway sprinted towards the young couple with her gun ready.

'Do not give me an excuse to shoot you,' she yelled.

Inside the fire door, Marion looked anxiously at Robin. 'Did that cop see us?'

'No idea,' Robin said, thinking about sneaking out the front exit on foot, but remembering there was a locked metal shutter.

'If she saw us, we're done for,' Marion said.

Robin grabbed his bow off the back of the bike. 'They might not have seen, but we can't take the chance.'

Outside, one cop fired a warning shot over the couple's heads as her colleague jumped out of his car.

'First and final warning,' the officer shouted. 'Hands behind heads!'

With two cops pointing guns from less than fifteen metres, the forest couple had to surrender.

'You wanna protest about Locksley Police?' the big guy said, pulling his baton as he strode in. 'I'll give you something to protest about.'

'They're cops with guns,' Marion blurted, as Robin slotted an arrow and slid two more between his fingers for rapid reloading. 'You can't take them on with that.'

'You might get push-ups at boot camp, but they'll hand me straight to Gisborne,' Robin said. 'Get on the bike and start the engine when I kick the door.'

Outside, the forest man groaned as the big cop smashed him with his baton.

'Forest scum,' the cop taunted, as he got ready to swing again. 'Got plenty more in store for –'

The back door flew open.

The big cop wore thick body armour over his torso, so Robin waited until the baton was raised high and shot him through the wrist. Before the man hit the ground, Robin had swung left and downed the female officer with an arrow through the top of her boot. She had enough fight to roll over and aim her gun, but Robin rushed out of the doorway and swung his bow to knock it out of her hand.

As Robin glanced warily, knowing there were more cops in the area, the forest woman grabbed the female officer's gun, then ordered the groaning male officer to hand over his car keys.

'You're Robin Hood,' her partner said disbelievingly, mouth bloody and dazed from his beating. 'That was unbelievable.'

'Can you walk?' the woman asked her boyfriend, as she kept the gun aimed at the groaning officers.

'Dead leg,' the guy answered.

'Piggyback,' the woman told him, going down on one knee, then looking at Robin. 'Do you need a ride?'

Robin shook his head before she waddled to the cop car with her boyfriend on her back.

Marion had already ridden the bike out of Captain Cash and Robin hopped on. She weaved around the wheezing cop with the arrow stuck through his wrist then accelerated hard.

The bow only left Robin with one hand to grab Marion, but the money bag bulging over the rear wheel saved him from tilting off the back.

'Careful!' he yelled, as the bike blasted away.

55. THE GOOD GUY ALWAYS HAS ONE SHOT LEFT

The driver of the hijacked police car gave Robin a thumbs up as she pulled onto Locksley High Street. Marion took a different path, aiming for the giant weeds up back, then cutting onto the overgrown plot behind.

Robin ducked as a bullet went off, but had no idea who was shooting or if he was the target. As they pulled onto one of the town centre's many barren side streets, the searchlight beam lit them up and the police SUV set off down the alleyway between Hipsta Donut and Captain Cash.

They had a three-hundred-metre start, but dirt bikes are designed for rough ground rather than speed, and they're slower still with two riders and luggage.

'Can't hold that monster off,' Marion said, looking for a narrow alleyway or some rough terrain as the SUV's chrome bull bars got bigger in her mirrors.

Robin glanced behind as the cop car closed to ten metres. He had the last of his three arrows in hand, but his family wasn't rich enough for ATVs, quad bikes or horses, so he had zero experience of shooting on the move.

He twisted around, clamped his legs as hard as he could to the bike and felt properly scared when he let go of Marion's waist. He figured two things. First, the police driver could easily make an evasive swerve if he took too long to aim. Second, the only way to disable a car with a single arrow was to shoot out a tyre.

'Veer into the opposite lane,' Robin shouted. 'I need an angle to shoot the front wheel.'

'There's got to be an alleyway around here,' Marion yelled back. 'Or a canal bank. Even a damned swing park . . .'

There was probably some regulation saying police officers weren't allowed to smash two twelve-year-olds with no helmets off a bike doing fifty miles an hour. But the driver didn't seem to care, flooring the accelerator as they hit a straight section of road in front of an abandoned cement works.

The front of the cop car was less than five metres behind when Marion swerved. Robin wasn't sure if she'd done it to help him shoot, or because the car was about to destroy them. Either way, he raised the bow and took aim.

The bike hit a pothole, delaying the shot. From less than five metres, the arrow went exactly where Robin wanted it. But it only nicked the SUV's spinning tyre before flipping up and getting sucked into the wheel arch.

'I don't think it punctured,' Robin yelled.

Marion knew they'd never win a straight race and took a sharp right turn. The heavy cop car had to slam the brakes to follow. But as the driver turned the wheel at speed, the sideways load turned the small hole Robin's arrow had made in the sidewall into a tear that split the entire tyre from its metal rim.

With the tyre flapping, all deceleration got thrown to the passenger side. The nose of the SUV dipped, tearing off its front fender and showering sparks. In panic the driver braked harder, but this locked the rear wheels and made the turn into a pirouette.

The SUV flipped when the nose hit a kerb. The flashing top lights got ripped away and the roof scraped along the sidewalk until a trash can smashed through the windscreen. It finally stopped after buckling a streetlamp and bouncing on the cement works' chain-link fence.

'We got lucky,' Marion said, as she felt Robin's hand slide back around her waist.

'Luck?' Robin laughed. 'That's exactly what I was going for.'

56. THE LONG WALK HOME

The trouble that started in Civic Square had spread throughout the populated parts of Locksley.

As Robin and Marion rode across town towards Sherwood, they saw buildings on fire and a group of city youths who'd looted a liquor store then turned vodka bottles into petrol bombs when the cops came.

Marion thought there might be Rangers blocking the major forest roads because of the trouble, so they rode a couple of kilometres up a busy Route 24 and pulled off at an unmarked exit that had once formed the start of a scenic walk.

The moonless forest was dark and the path heavily overgrown. They abandoned the bike after four hundred metres, rolling it away from the path and tearing up ferns to hide it.

'This is as close as we'll get a bike to Designer Outlets,' Marion said.

'You reckon it'll be here when we come back?'

Marion shrugged. 'Someone might stumble on it, but it's a big forest.'

Their eyes adjusted to the dark as they swapped sneakers for boots and split the money so they both carried the same load. Robin was amazed at how Marion navigated a kilometre of black forest, locating a dribbling stream. After a brisk fifty-minute walk, where the water never topped their boots, they met the more powerful stream they'd wound up in two nights earlier.

Neither of them fancied wading, so Marion found a crossing that was a mix of stepping stones and a precarious walk over two rotting logs. Once they were across, they could see Designer Outlets' south parking lot, and Marion pulled out her radio to let the watchtower know they were coming in.

It took half a minute for a guard to open a steel-plated door, then they stepped into the southernmost tip of the H-shaped mall. Nobody lived down this end because it regularly flooded and there was a muggy, mushroom, smell.

'This is my cousin, Freya Tuck,' Marion introduced. Then to Freya, 'I thought you'd be in town throwing rocks through windows.'

'Worst night to draw guard duty,' Freya complained. 'I've heard the whole of Locksley has kicked off.'

'Pretty much,' Marion nodded, then broke into a huge yawn.

'I need my bed,' she said. 'I'm trashed.'

'You wish,' Freya grinned, as Robin caught the yawn. 'I've got orders to take you up to Will's command tent. He's cheesed off with you guys going AWOL.'

'Freya, let us sneak up to bed,' Marion begged. 'I can handle Will in the morning.'

'He heard your radio call,' Freya said, shaking her head. 'He's expecting you.'

57. STEAL FROM THE RICH, GIVE TO THE POOR

Will ran Designer Outlets from his sand-coloured command tent directly beneath the three-storey watchtower.

The inside was hung with maps of the mall and surrounding forest, detailed plans of electrical and plumbing systems and an enormous whiteboard with rotas for everything from guard duty to tending rooftop vegetable gardens.

'Sit,' Will growled, snapping his fingers from behind a desk as Freya led the pair in.

Indio was there and Marion got a *thank-God-you're-alive* hug, followed by a finger-wagging scowl.

'The next time you decide not to answer my calls or reply to my voice messages, I might decide that you don't need a phone!'

'I'm sorry,' Marion said guiltily, backing away from her mum and settling into the seat next to Robin.

'I've had search teams out looking for you,' Will said

angrily. 'Karma and Indio have been worried sick. When you set off, we assumed you were a lot more responsible than this. It is *never* acceptable to stay out of touch when we call you.'

'If you want to be treated like adults, you have to act like adults,' Indio added. 'Maybe I should send you to live with your dad for a while. You'll be a lot worse than grounded if you break Cut-Throat's rules.'

Robin and Marion looked awkwardly at one another until Will pounded on the table.

'Did Gisborne cut out your tongues?' he asked. 'And what's with the leggings and unicorn?'

'Stop smirking,' Indio growled.

'I'm not smirking.' Marion smirked, as Robin reached into his backpack and placed a six-centimetre wodge of hundred-pound notes on Will's desk.

When Marion saw his stunned reaction, she reached down into her bag and did the same.

'I haven't done an accurate count,' Robin said softly. 'But it's roughly a hundred and twenty.'

'Thousand,' Marion added.

Now the grown-ups did stunned silence while Robin found his voice.

'I need ten to pay to Tybalt for Dad's legal costs,' Robin began. 'I think me and Marion should be allowed to each keep ten for ourselves, cos we don't exactly have rich parents and we'll need stuff as we grow.

'The other ninety is for Designer Outlets. The clinic,

the library, education programmes . . .'

'Maybe get the night-vision goggles you want for the watchtower,' Marion suggested.

The pair kept stacking money as they spoke until Will could barely see their faces over the mound.

'I'm really sorry I ignored your calls and made you all worry,' Marion said. 'But we needed to do this, and I knew you'd say no.'

'I'll take whatever punishment,' Robin added. 'Ground me. Make me dig vegetables or clean toilets. Just don't kick me out, because you people are all I have.'

Will fanned some of the notes and almost smiled as he broke silence. 'This money will make a huge difference. But where did it come from?'

Before Robin or Marion could answer, Indio started blubbing.

'I'm so touched that you did . . . whatever you did . . . to help out,' she sniffled as she wrapped her arms around Marion. 'But I was *so* scared that Gisborne had got you, and no amount of money could *ever* compensate for losing you.'

Marion's eyes glazed with tears as Indio stepped sideways, making Robin feel loved as she hugged him too.

'Same goes for you, Robin,' Indio said. 'But you *know* we'd never kick a child out of here, so don't come at me with the puppy-dog face . . .'

'Am I still grounded?' Marion asked, glancing up cheekily.

'I'll reduce it by half,' Indio said, unable to hide a smile as tears streaked her face. 'You were grounded for two hundred years, now it's just one hundred.'

Will had moist eyes too, but he spoke seriously. 'I appreciate what you've done, but you *can't* go gallivanting without letting adults know.'

'No more crazy adventures,' Indio said firmly. 'I'll let you off this time. But you *both* have to promise.'

'I promise,' Marion sighed. 'Sorry, Mum.'

Robin nodded in agreement. 'No more adventures, *ever.*'

But of course, they both had their fingers crossed.

EPILOGUE – THE LEGEND OF ROBIN HOOD

'Good evening, this is Channel Fourteen serving the Central Region. I'm Lynn Hoapili with a specially extended evening news.

'The City of Locksley awoke in a state of shock this morning, to broken glass, smouldering buildings, more than fifty arrests and a dozen wounded law-enforcement officers.

'For some, last night's events were a terrorist outrage, sparked by a car exploding inside Locksley Central Court, and further proof that rebels and refugees in Sherwood Forest are out of control.

'For others, the violence was an inevitable result of Sheriff Marjorie Kovacevic's increasingly harsh policies, which critics say demonise and discriminate against Forest People.

'But when we spoke to people on the streets of Locksley today, there was just one name on everyone's lips.

'Twelve-year-old Locksley High pupil Robin Hood escaped into the forest just one week ago, following an incident that ended with the shooting of controversial local businessman Guy Gisborne.

'While last night's rioting took place, Hood is believed to have disguised himself as a girl and robbed two ATMs for more than £100,000. The pint-sized thief then escaped on a motorbike after wounding two police officers.

'A CCTV camera mounted in the car park of a neighbouring donut store caught footage of Hood's dramatic escape and a balletic display of speed archery that already has more than twelve million online views.

'Earlier today, Channel Fourteen went to Locksley High School and spoke with two of Robin's classmates, Stephanie Trump and Tiffany Stalin.'

The bulletin cut to a shot of two girls in too much make-up and Locksley High polo shirts.

'I always thought Robin was cool,' Stephanie told the camera. 'Like, a total bad boy . . . But, like, I guess . . . Like, even cool people can't rob ATMs and shoot cops with arrows.'

'I loved that unicorn hoodie in the CCTV,' Tiffany added, before giggling and looking at her friend. 'It's awesome that he's in touch with his feminine side.'

Stephanie nodded. 'I tried buying one online for my boyfriend, but it's sold out everywhere.'

Lynn Hoapili did a voiceover, as the image cut from the two girls to a big man in a bad tie. 'Robin's Head of Year, Joseph Barclay, also gave us his thoughts:'

'Robin is a very able pupil,' Mr Barclay began. 'He got into a few scrapes, but he's basically a nice kid.

'We've now got "Robin Hood Lives" written all over our school. I can't condone graffiti, or assault, but I think Robin has become a symbol of the frustration Locksley High pupils feel at everything, from education cuts to getting harassed by corrupt cops on the street and seeing Forest People die because they can't get hospital treatment.'

The report cut back to Lynn in the studio.

'Other people we spoke to in Locksley today pointed out that Robin symbolises unity. A city boy who crossed the divide and moved into the forest. And while the Sheriff of Nottingham has often blamed Forest People for problems in her county, last night's protests were notable for involving Locksley residents and multiple forest groups.

'But while some see Robin Hood as a youthful hero, and mascot for a burgeoning protest movement, the head of Locksley Police Department, Karen Thomas, made it clear she did not share these feelings.'

The broadcast cut to a mean-looking cop with lots of gold braid on her uniform.

'Last night's terrorist action, the subsequent

rioting and the violent robbery committed by Robin Hood has caused millions of pounds in damage, frightened ordinary citizens and left seven of Locksley's decent, hardworking police officers in the hospital,' Chief Thomas began.

'As of now, I am officially putting Robin Hood at the number-one spot on Locksley's Most Wanted list. And to those who think that someone who shot and wounded a well-respected businessman and two of my officers is a hero, I say this:

'Robin Hood will be caught. And when that happens, his punishment will be severe.'

Look out for

PIRACY, PAINTBALLS & ZEBRAS

Read on for an extract . . .

NEWS UPDATE

'Good afternoon, this is Channel Fourteen serving the Central Region. I'm Lynn Hoapili with your local headlines.

'Our top story is that traffic on Route 24 is still subject to severe delays after a tyre blew out on a truck filled with zebras during this morning's rush hour. The vehicle rolled onto its side and the rear doors flew open as it smashed into the central barrier.

'Eyewitnesses described scenes of chaos as weak and filthy zebras escaped the truck and stumbled into twelve lanes of busy traffic. Several vehicles crashed as they swerved to avoid the animals. Five motorists were taken to hospital by air ambulance and while most of the animals fled into surrounding forest, vets had to destroy one zebra that was hit by a car.

'A spokesperson for the Animal Freedom Militia

has claimed the zebras were being shipped to Sherwood Castle for an upcoming trophy hunt and that cramming so many animals into a small truck is a serious breach of animal welfare regulations. Sherwood Castle management has so far refused to comment.

'In other news, there has been a surprise twist in the controversial trial of Ardagh Hood. Moments before his case went before a judge, Hood accepted a plea deal. In return for a three-year prison sentence, the Locksley man pled guilty to the theft of laptop computers and to resisting arrest.

'Scuffles broke out when news of the guilty plea reached Ardagh's supporters outside court, and police made several arrests. Hood's lawyer, Tybalt Bull, said he would have liked to continue the fight to prove Ardagh's innocence, but that his client risked a sixteen-year prison sentence if he had been found guilty after a full trial.

'Those are the noon headlines. I'll be back with our main bulletin at one o'clock.'

1. PINT-SIZED TEARAWAY

Sherwood Forest stretched across the land, from Lake Victoria to the swampy Eastern Delta. Twenty thousand square kilometres, inhabited by bears, snakes, gigantic crunchy-shelled bugs and a vast population of yellow birds that lived nowhere else on Earth.

Estimates of Sherwood's human population varied between thirty thousand and a quarter of a million, and most of them were hiding from something. Bandits, bikers, religious cults, terrorists, refugees and one twelve-year-old boy with a £100,000 bounty on his head.

To find Robin Hood you had to travel eight kilometres north from his birth town of Locksley, take a right off the twelve-lane Route 24 expressway, then hike down a road that had mostly been reclaimed by forest until you reached the parking lots of Sherwood Designer Outlet Mall.

It was more than a decade since the sprawling mall sold its last bargain kitchenware and discounted handbags.

Now the abandoned H-shaped shopping centre housed a well-organised outlaw community, protected by trip wires, motion alarms and armed guards stationed on a precarious wooden observation tower.

Although it was just after one on a spring afternoon, Robin Hood had taken to his den on the upper level of an abandoned sporting-goods outlet. The den was eight by six metres, with walls made from wobbly shop partitions. He sprawled face down on a musty but comfortable mattress, buried under oversized cushions, two duvets and a Berber rug.

Robin's bestie, Marion Maid, had been sent upstairs to tell him lunch was ready. She only realised he was under the mound of bedding because a couple of grubby toes poked out.

'Hey, pal,' Marion said quietly, as she knelt by the bed. 'Everyone's about to eat.'

'Don't feel like it,' Robin said.

His words were clipped because he didn't want Marion to hear that he was upset. Normally she'd have dived into the cushions or grabbed Robin's ankle and tickled his foot. But today was different.

'I'm really sorry about your dad,' she said.

'I can't even visit him without getting busted,' Robin complained. 'My mum's dead. And my big brother is living in luxury at Sherwood Castle with his new mommy.'

'You've got me,' Marion said. 'And everyone here has your back.'

4

Robin didn't respond, so she tried a different tactic. Unfortunately it came out sounding grumpier than she meant it to.

'What are you gonna do? Stay under that mound of covers for the rest of your life?'

'I can try,' Robin snapped back.

'If you can't face everyone, how about I bring a plate up? This afternoon we can watch a movie on Netflix. Take your mind off things.'

'Internet's down,' Robin said. 'And there's *nothing* to do. I'm totally bored and I'm not allowed out of the mall.'

'What are we supposed to do? With a hundred-thousand bounty on your head, every scumbag in Sherwood Forest will be after you.'

Marion watched the mound of covers shift slightly. Dust billowed as the rug slid onto the floor and she smiled as Robin sat up, sweaty and shirtless. His eyes were gluey from crying and his hair was even messier than usual.

'What's funny?' Robin asked, as he stretched and yawned.

'You look adorable,' Marion teased, as she spotted Robin's T-shirt on the floor and flicked it towards him. 'Like a lost puppy.'

'I'm actually kinda starving,' Robin admitted, a bit more cheerful as his head popped through the neck hole of his shirt.

'You're always starving,' Marion said.

'Growing boy,' Robin said, slapping his belly, then

creasing up his nose. 'Why do you stink of fish?'

'Went fishing with my cousin Freya,' Marion said, as she sniffed her hoodie. 'Must have got splattered when we were gutting them.'

Robin looked sour as he stood up. 'Thanks for inviting me.'

'We didn't invite you cos you can't leave the mall without guards,' Marion said, as Robin pulled on wrecked Vans.

'I can't hack another week sitting around here, with nothing but schoolwork and your aunt Lucy's sudoku books,' Robin said. 'I need an adventure – like busting my dad out of jail.'

Marion laughed. 'We're twelve, and Pelican Island is the most secure prison in the country. So ten out of ten for ambition, but a fat zero for practicality.'

'So I sit around here, getting older, doing nothing?'

'We get bossed around by grown-ups, do boring schoolwork and try to have fun when we can,' Marion said. 'That's basically what being a kid is.'

'Who wants to be an ordinary kid?' Robin asked determinedly as he grabbed the carbon-fibre bow hooked on the wall beside his bed. 'I'm not ordinary, I'm Robin Hood.'

Robert Muchamore's books have sold 15 million copies in over 30 countries, been translated into 24 languages and been number-one bestsellers in eight countries including the UK, France, Germany, Australia and New Zealand.

Find out more at
muchamore.com

Follow Robert
on Facebook and Twitter
@RobertMuchamore

Discover more books and sign up to the Robert Muchamore mailing list at muchamore.com

 muchamore

 muchamorerobert

 @robertmuchamore

HOT
KEY
BOOKS

Thank you for choosing a Hot Key book.

If you want to know more about our authors
and what we publish, you can find us online.

You can start at our website

www.hotkeybooks.com

And you can also find us on:

We hope to see you soon!